HAZEL HALLEY
AND
THE PLANET OF RINGS

Written and Illustrated By

KHUSHI GOEL

INDIA • SINGAPORE • MALAYSIA

ISBN 979-8-89067-998-7

Disclaimer

CONTENTS

ACKNOWLEDGEMENTS

I'm deeply indebted to my parents as nothing would have been possible without their persevering support. I thank God for blessing me with the most motivating parents. You both are my inspiration to work hard. You always give me ideas, show me the path and help fulfil all my dreams.

My gratitude to my Grandparents whose stories instilled the art of story-telling in me. Thank you Dadi-Dadu and Nani-Nanu for your infinite love, kindness and wisdom.

I am grateful to all my teachers for nurturing me with their erudite advice and showing me the way.

My heartfelt gratitude to Uncle Afsar Baig (Midland Book Shop, Haus Khas, New Delhi). Your support, positivity and encouragement gave me the strength I needed to take these steps towards my dream of becoming an author. Mere words can never express my gratitude to you.

A BIG THANK YOU TO ALL MY READERS FOR PICKING UP THIS BOOK!

HOPE YOU ENJOY READING MY NOVELS!

CHAPTER ONE
SUMMER HOLIDAYS

Last year, Hazel Halley, the girl with dark brown hair and twinkly hazel eyes fought the Comet of Ice. The comet attacked her best friend Hannah Hope and she had enough. She flared up and marched right into Space, fighting the comet herself. Hazel returned victorious to Earth with the help of her new friends who lived on the Moon…

Now, it was summer holidays and she was back in her enormous house, which consisted of six bedrooms.

"Dad, did I tell you that I was selected for the school Surfwink team last week?" asked Hazel.

"No," replied Mr. Halley.

"I'm a Catcher because I chased the Comet of Ice." Hazel said.

"What comet?" asked Mrs. Halley.

"Err..." mumbled Hazel. Mrs. Halley would faint if she found out about her daughter's adventure. "The tiny plastic model comets that zoom in the school." Hazel fibbed.

Hazel managed to lie about her ginormous adventure by telling her parents that she wasn't missing, but her friend was and that imaginary 'friend' was the one who stopped the comet.

"So proud," beamed Mrs. Halley.

"Anyway, do you know what summer holidays mean?" asked Mr. Halley.

"No," said Hazel, chewing her toast.

"FAMILY CAMP!" he grinned. His eyes twinkled as he combed his dark hair. He wore an elegant coat which made him look very handsome.

Hazel hated family camp. Her father felt cold; and forced everyone to wear a jacket too so Hazel had to put up with rashes and the sweltering heat.

Mr. Halley had two left feet when it came to camping. Fay was whining and crying of how this would affect her studies. Holly was always up to mischief, giving her dad a hard time. The twins were after their mum's life to do camp activities. Mrs. Halley would always take everyone on very long nature walks.

"Oh dear, why do I think this is not going to turn up the way dad expects it," she whispered.

"Yay! I'm off to pack then!" Holly smiled, knowing how much Hazel hated camp.

"We should start packing now. Pack a warm coat and an extra jumper. No Holly, not that pink one as it has a broken button, the big warm fuzzy purple one I knitted last Christmas." Mrs. Halley announced.

It was Holly's turn to groan. She hated wearing layers of clothes and socks. The purple jumper was too large and absolutely hideous with that bunny knitted in the middle saying 'I love my mommy'.

"How many tents do we have?" Ava asked.

"Holly blew up one or two tents last year. So me and your mum will share one tent, you twins can share one, Hazel and Holly can have another and Fay can have the last one." Mr. Halley said.

"What about Annie?" Fay asked.

HOLLY HALLEY

"How come you have your own tent?" snapped Anna.

"Fay can share her tent with Annie, is that alright honey?" Mrs. Halley asked. Anna nodded.

"I'll be in charge of the food and drinks!" Hazel grinned.

"I'll put the tents up and Anna can place the sleeping bags." Ava giggled.

"Fay you will manage Annie. Carry her nappies, bibs and bottles since you will be sharing your tent with her." Mrs. Halley said.

Fay turned red, embarrassed. Holly and Hazel sniggered.

"I'll set up the fire!" Mr. Halley smiled.

"I will carry things like flashlights, binoculars and bug spray." Holly said.

"Alright, all settled then." Mrs. Halley told.

"And don't forget it's my birthday next week!" Hazel smiled.

"We won't forget, I have arranged a little surprise for you too, honey bun." Mrs. Halley said.

FAY ANDD ANNE HALLEY

"What's the surprise?" Hazel eagerly asked. "It wouldn't be a surprise if I told you, would it? You'll just have to wait."

Now Hazel was excited to go. She smiled eagerly and trooped into her room.

She opened her spacious yellow camping bag and started packing right away. Mrs. Halley came in her pink and white room.

"Any questions," Mrs. Halley asked, "About the camping holiday?"

"Erm… I have one, no, two questions. First, when will we leave?" Hazel asked.

"Tomorrow," Mrs. Halley replied.

"Secondly, where are we camping? Not the Wispy Woods, according to my calculations, those woods are facing floods, plus those bare trees give me the creeps." Hazel shuddered.

"Well, we're actually going to the Seven Hills. Seven tall lush green hills were named the Seven Hills, and it is the perfect place to camp. There is so much beauty, greenery, peace and there are so many positive vibes there, you feel so relaxed and peaceful. We will camp at the top of the fourth hill." Mrs. Halley said.

"How many days are we going there?" inquired Hazel.

"Two or three weeks, I wanted it to be a month really. But Fay cut our trip short. Now we will go for two weeks. We'll have so much fun. I'm carrying all the food as well and a chocolate cake for your special day too. I simply love what I planned for the menu," grinned Mrs. Halley.

"Thanks mum, I better start packing then." Hazel smiled. Mrs. Halley went out of the room.

"Picnic blanket, check. Sleeping bag, clothes, swimming costume, all check." Hazel mumbled as the ticked things off a long checklist she was holding with a green marker.

She finally packed everything in her bag. She even remembered to carry an umbrella, her coat and an extra jumper.

"Goodness me! How will I fit in the tent?" Hazel exclaimed. "Looks like I have to give this to Ava. Do I need any entertainment? Dad'll manage that, I'm sure."

"Hazel!" came Holly's voice from her room.

"Yes?" said Hazel.

"Would you be a dear and help me pack my stuff if you're done. I could use a little help." Holly implored.

"Coming!" Hazel cried out and marched into Holly's room.

"Oh Holly, what in the name of pickle cheese did you do?" Hazel exclaimed, flabbergasted.

"I got in a pickle myself," chuckled Holly.

Her room was a mess. Everything was scattered all around. Hazel could hardly see the ground. It was impossible to walk there!

"Alright, clothes in the cupboard, food in the kitchen, tricks in the trick box, school stuff on the study table, books on the book shelf and camping stuff in the camping bag!" Hazel instructed as Holly cleaned up.

"Now it's time see how Fay's getting along," Hazel giggled and entered Fay's room.

"Books, books and more books. Packed. Papers, pens, books, books and more books." Fay mumbled while she was packing.

"What about your clothes and flashlight and bug spray?" Hazel asked.

"I forgot!" Fay said, packing the other stuff required under Hazel's instructions.

"And Annie's own bag. Bibs, binky, bottles, clothes, napkins, milk, food, clothes, Bubby her stuffed bunny and a toy or two should be enough to keep her happy." Hazel told.

"Thanks Hazel," whispered Fay.

"WAAH!" came a wail.

"Calm down!" shouted Hazel. Annie wailed harder. It was pandemonium. "WAAH!"

"Fine then, thanks Hazel. Now I better give Annie's binky to her." Fay whispered and gave Annie her binky.

Hazel went to everyone's room and helped them out.

"Change of plans! Girls, if we leave now; we would reach by morning." Mrs. Halley said, looking at the clock.

"Are we ready?" Mr. Halley asked.

"Yes," Anna replied.

"Then let's go!" Mr. Halley exclaimed and the Halleys dragged their bags on the street.

The air was pleasant and cool. Flowers bloomed and the leaves of the trees were swaying merrily with the wind. The road was big and broad. All the elegant white houses on the street were spacious and very fancy with front yards.

"Hi Georgie!" a voice came. A young man was walking on the road, dragging a pink pram. A girl was walking alongside.

He had dark wavy hair like Mr. Halley and his eyes were like Hazel's. This man had a warm smile on his face and looked as if he went to the gym every day.

The baby in the pink pram was less than a year old. She had a tuft of black hair, green eyes and chubby cheeks. Some saliva was dribbling out of her mouth.

The other girl had a round face with olive green skin. Her hair were tied in two pigtails with blue ribbon. She was also wearing a frock over her white shirt. This girl's name was Sally.

"Hello Frank," Mr. Halley smiled. This man was his friendly neighbour and they knew each other quite well. "Hi Sally and hello baby Lucy, how are you?" he asked.

"Fine, fine, where are yeh going Georgie?" Frank asked.

"Camp," Mr. Halley said.

"Was a boy scout myself, yeh were the worst camper in those days." Frank said.

"That was long time ago," Mr. Halley replied, gruffly.

"See yeh Georgie," Frank smiled.

"Bye Frank!" Mr. Halley said and marched off towards his daughters.

"Bye uncle!" Sally called out. "Bye to you too Sally, have a great day." Mr. Halley answered.

Just then, they could hear an engine purr. A camper van had come!

This van was the size of a mini bus which was yellow in colour. It was really tall and had big rubber tyres.

A driver who had tanned skin was sitting on the driver's seat. He had small gooseberry eyes and pink blubbery lips. His fat belly jiggled like jelly on the bumps.

"Hello, is this the 'alley family I see?" he asked in a deep voice. It was manly, rough and rasping.

"It's us alright," grunted Mrs. Halley.

"There yeh go. Hey George, here are yeh keys. Don't lose 'em," the driver said, giving him the keys.

"Thanks," Mr. Halley said, bluntly.

"Yeh the last man I expected to see 'ere goin' to camp out fer weeks. Frank told me yeh the wors' camper in the world."

Mr. Halley grunted, "I might need to have a word with Frank, then."

Hazel giggled.

"Have fun!" the driver said in a more friendly tone.

Mr. Halley, clearly disliking this man more by the minute, climbed the van and sat on the driver's recliner seat; large and comfortable.

Mrs. Halley sat beside him, holding a map. Fay jumped aboard dragging Annie's pushchair. Holly leapt in with Fay's trunk, and her own. The twins entered carrying their own bags and dragging Annie's baby bag as well. Hazel hopped aboard.

It was nothing like a mini bus from inside; there were no seats! There was a kitchen towards Hazel's left, the slab was made of expensive Italian tiles. There was a sink to wash utensils in and a stove to cook things on.

A bathroom with a big tub and a shower on her right. The lobby had a dining table in the centre and sofa to sit on.

Hazel was surprised to see there were stairs leading her up. She climbed up the flight of stairs.

Upstairs were bedrooms with fluffy beds. But they were small in size so only one person could sleep on it.

CHAPTER TWO

THE WORST TRIP EVER

Fay took the bed and Annie bawled in her cradle. Fay least bothered to give Annie her bottle and started reading her Reflections book, grade five.

The parents were driving. Ava took the bed and Anna set her sleeping bag on the floor. Hazel jumped on the bed and said, "I bags this bed," before Holly could hog up the bed for herself.

"Too late," came Holly's swift reply.

"What!" said Hazel. "I came here first!"

"Don't yeh see my bag is kept on the side table, I have the bed." Holly grinned.

"Well, your bag is kept on the side table so you can sleep on it. I'm taking the bed!" Hazel fumed.

"A game of Snap will decide who gets the bed," ordered Holly.

She shuffled and divided the cards. The game had begun.

Hazel threw an orange fish card; Holly threw the card with a red ball and so on…

A purple flower; a yellow Sun; a green parrot; a brown triangle; a pink bird; an orange tiger; a white snowflake; a black balloon; a red toffee; a blue rectangle; a blue square; a green square; a red square; a red square...

"Snap! I win!" cheered Holly. The game continued.

Grey comb; green beetle; yellow tennis racket; a yellow tennis racket…

"I win this time!" grinned Hazel.

"That game was quick. One last," demanded Holly.

Pink butterfly; brown puppy; purple poppies; a red plant; green rose; green rose…

"I win and I get the bed!" roared Holly.

"No you don't," bellowed Hazel.

The fight continued.

"Yes too."

"No not."

"Yes!"

"No!"

"Yes, yes!"

"No, no!"

"Yesses!"

"Nooooo!"

"Yes!"

"Alright, I give in. You get the bed." Hazel sighed.

Holly smiled. "Fooled you again! I didn't keep any bag on the bed, so if you kept protesting, we wouldn't have played Snap and you would've got the bed. Too bad, hahahahaha!" she cackled.

Hazel completely lost it.

"Nooo! You little wretch! You're an absolute beast, Holly."

Holly bounced on her bed. "I'll help you put up your sleeping bag."

"No way!" Hazel said, completely fed up and utterly disgusted. Her own sister had cheated her!

She set up her own sleeping bag by herself. Holly watched and sniggered.

Hazel cursed her fluently under her breath. She put Polly's cage by the window. Polly the parrot merrily squawked.

She spent the rest of her night sleeping without dinner. She had no wish left to stay awake a minute longer.

It was now dawn. Hazel woke up with a fresh start. Holly was sleeping; she was a night owl. Hazel thought of a spiteful trick to play on her.

She picked up Holly's trumpet and screamed, "GOOOOD MORNIIIIING!"

"AAH!" Holly screamed.

"We have arrived! Toodle pip!" Hazel yelled as she packed her bag and went out of the room. She locked the door.

"Get me out of here or I'll tell mum!" Holly bellowed.

"You got what you deserved; the bed was mine and it still is!" Hazel snapped.

"Mum! Hazel's locked me in!" cried Holly.

Hazel could hear the thundering footsteps of her mother, which were seriously louder and more dangerous than an earthquake.

"Okay, I'll unlock you on condition that I get the bed on the way back." Hazel hastily said, unlocking the door.

The Halleys trotted off the camper van. They had arrived!

"Wow! This is, this is beautiful." Hazel cooed, admiring the beauty of the Seven Hills.

"I agree, how fun will the nature walks here be, I wonder." Mrs. Halley agreed.

The Seven Hills were paradise for her. They were at the bottom of the fourth hill. The hill was like a mountain, towering and tall. The grass was lush green in colour and tiny yellow buttercups with dew drops on the field made the ground glitter like jewels.

A stream with fresh, cool and pristine water flowed past them. The day was warm and sunny with the breeze passing by.

Colourful butterflies flapped their delicate wings and settled on the field of roses. Adorable bunnies bounced by, their whiskers twitching.

The limpid dewdrops clinging to the speckled leaves,

The morning air, the pleasant breeze,

And the cobbled path that cleaves,

The far stretched plains of fertile land,

It was like a fairytale land,

The lupins and lavenders,

and so many flowers,

The grass dancing in the early morning showers,

The water gurgles as it rushes down the stream,

The poppies unfurl like pictures of a dream,

The colourful birds chirp as their spirits fly,

Leaving behind the dazzling rainbow hanging in the sky!

"I want one of those bunnies and I won't leave till I get one!" said Anna, firmly.

"Me too! Fay has a raven, Holly has a macaw and Hazel has Polly; I want a pet Daddy, so get me one." Ava said.

"You will get your pets when you are eleven!" Mrs. Halley replied, equally firm.

"Come on, there's not really that much harm in getting a bunny." Mr. Halley said.

Mrs. Halley nodded. "Then I'll set up the camp. Holly, try making boiled eggs, strips of bacon, tomato salad with cucumbers mixed with cream cheese, honey sandwiches and arrange a bottle of milk as well. Two bottles, in fact." Mr. Halley said.

Ava and Anna hugged him tight and went bunny hunting.

"Well, looks like your dad is busy. Holly, prepare the food. Fay, spread the picnic blanket. Hazel, be Holly's assistant." Mrs. Halley ordered.

Holly went in the camper van to cook some food in the kitchen. Hazel trotted after her.

"Alright Hazel. We are going to cook in this cramped-up kitchen. Then dad will set up camp and we can park this rusty van further down the hill so we don't see its ugly face again till we need to go back. And I don't know how to cook, so you be the main chef." Holly explained.

"We wash our hands first. When was the last time you did?" Hazel told her.

"Only a week ago! They're perfectly clean!" Holly insisted.

Hazel wrinkled her nose. "That's disgusting! What's that sticky thing?"

"Just a wad of mouldy chewing gum and... oh, I get it. I'll go wash."

"Wise choice."

Holly came back, her hands thankfully clean.

"Now we can cook. Boil the eggs, heat up the milk, chop the cucumbers and tomatoes, or love apples, as I call them. I'll do the rest," she ordered.

Holly dropped the eggs. "Never mind," said Hazel. Holly spilled the milk. "Be careful or I'll tell mum." Hazel warned.

"How does mum boil eggs?" she asked.

"I don't know!" snapped Hazel. "We should crack them and fry it instead. We can serve omlette."

Holly prepared the omlette. Hazel mixed the roughly chopped tomatoes and cucumber with cream cheese and made a salad. She cut the edges of the bread and put a thick layer of honey on it. Finally, Hazel prepared some strips of bacon and wrapped it in grease proof paper.

"What will we drink?" asked Holly.

"There is no milk right now, I forgot. I have a bottle of lime cordial and grape juice." Hazel answered.

Holly carried everything and put it on the red and white picnic blanket.

"The salad vegetables are in a crazy shape; I can't grip it to my fork!" Fay complained.

"But everything else is delicious," Mrs. Halley commented.

Hazel munched on her honey sandwiches quietly, and drank the lime cordial in one gulp.

"We're back!" came Mr. Halley's voice, panting. The twins looked miserable.

"We couldn't catch them; they jumped in their burrows!" pouted Anna.

"It's okay, you'll get a pet next year anyway!"

"Let's set up camp now," Mr. Halley said.

"Okay daddy," giggled Hazel. They climbed the hill, which looked more like a mountain.

Hazel and Holly, stuck together like glue on the trip, set up a red tent. The parents had a blue tent; the twins shared the yellow tent and Fay had the green one. Another large blue tent was set up for the kitchen and to keep their luggage.

"Why can we sleep in the van?" asked Hazel.

"Bedbugs," groaned Mr. Halley.

He stated that it would be more prudent to sleep in a tent and 'connect with nature'.

"If it's a rainy night, we'd have to sleep in there." Fay added, disgruntled. She hated the 'great outdoors'.

"Oh my, daddy!" Hazel exclaimed. "Your tent is upside down! You put up the tent poles backwards and nailed the whole thing upside down. The pegs are ripping your tent, and they are supposed to be hammered to the ground, not the tent!"

(Please don't think I don't know how to camp. It's not *my* fault that Mr. Halley is pants at camping!)

"Whoops, we blew up another tent! Well, we'll sleep in Fay's tent, to look after Annie." Mr. Halley said, wincing as Mrs. Halley tenderly kissed Annie and planted a kiss on Fay's cheek.

"Yuck, I'm in the tent if you need me. One needs to look after Annie." Fay lied and ran towards her tent. She actually wanted to read a book.

"Shall we head over to the stream? We can warm up and swim there too. Your mum can go to the farm and get some fresh food. That would be more healthy than tinned food which will rot after a few days." Mr. Halley suggested.

"A marvellous idea." Mr. Halley grinned as she grabbed a basket and went to the farm, waving goodbye.

Mr. Halley and the four girls changed into their swimming costumes and walked towards the stream on their tippy toes.

Hazel was about to do a graceful double flip dive into the stream when she received a rough push and fell in the stream. She managed to save herself just in time before she drowned.

"Holly!" she fumed. Holly didn't reply but jumped in the stream as well. The water temperature was immaculate. So pleasant, neither too hot or cold.

"Let's have races!" said Anna. "It'll be loads of fun."

"Yes!" cried the others.

The first was a normal race, and Hazel won that easily.

"I'm the champ, I'm the champ!" Hazel boasted.

"What a conceited pig," whispered Holly.

"I'm hungry, I want food!" bawled Ava.

"Come on then, your mum would be back by now." Mr. Halley said, wrapping his children in towels.

Mrs. Halley prepared the food in the kitchen tent.

Fresh scones, salad, cottage cheese, chicken, iced buns, raspberry pie, ham and salmon was waiting for them. Spreading the picnic blanket again, they all ate. Hazel munched on her scones, piece of pie, salad, cottage cheese and drank some freshly squeezed orange juice.

"What should we do now?" Mrs. Halley asked.

"Let's just relax, have a short nap." Holly said, relaxing on the grass and in soaking the Sun.

"Yes, let's do that." Mr. Halley said, lying down. The entire family lay down like Holly. The Sun was so inviting.

Hazel gazed at the splendid view for a fraction of a second, before falling asleep.

"An earthquake!" Hazel screamed. She heard a horrific thud and BAM! The ground was shaking and vibrating and it ripped into two!

"Everyone! Stay calm! Just stop moving! The vibration will stop soon! Don't speak at all! " Hazel shouted. Pin drop silence. Not a single movement. Soon after, the vibration stopped.

"What was that?" asked a frightened Ava.

"An earthquake, silly!" explained Fay. "When the plates of the Earth bang together, they create earthquakes!"

"I hate 'em," groaned Anna.

"Me too," said Fay. "Me too..."

CHAPTER THREE

"MY PANTS ARE ON FIRE!"

"Let's carry our stuff to the fifth hill, it will be much safer there." Mrs. Halley squeaked.

Every one hurried and quickly packed their bags and started their journey to reach the fifth hill.

"Water... I need water..." Hazel panted weakly, out of breath. She gulped down all the water. Every last drop in her bottle.

"Good, let's set up camp again," sighed Mr. Halley.

"Let's have supper first," Holly implored.

"No way! You just had lunch!" Mrs. Halley snapped.

"But the hiking made me hungry again!" protested Holly.

"Ava, would you be so kind enough to serve a glass of mango juice to everyone here?" Mrs. Halley asked.

"How?" asked Ava.

"Just take seven glasses, pour the bottle of mango juice in it and put in some crushed ice cubes." Anna panted.

"This juice is top notch, Ava. What did you put in it?" Hazel asked.

"Well," Ava girlishly giggled. "I may have spritzed a little bit of raspberry juice to enhance the flavour."

"Genius move."

"Nice juice, Ava, but now let's set up camp," groaned Mr. Halley.

The tired family set up camp as slowly as they could. Hazel didn't have the strength to tell that her father put his tent backwards this time.

"Oof!" Holly moaned.

"Let's go for a very long nature walk." Mrs. Halley beamed.

"My dear, none of us here can walk a single mile, let alone a nature walk. We are all so tired right now." Mr. Halley said.

"Then what shall we do till supper?" asked Ava.

"Read a book!" Mrs. Halley said.

Hazel loathed reading. Everything went wrong today, sleeping on the bug-infected floor and now reading? This was the worst camp ever!

"I'm sure you'd love *Moby Dick*!" Holly persuaded her, giving Hazel a very thick book, knowing she despised reading.

Hazel read some of the chapters, which made her sick to her stomach. She scowled at Holly. "I hope you enjoy reading Shakespeare's *Merchant of Venice*, or *Anne of Green Gables*. Whatever. Rebecca said they're awesome."

"If Rebecca said that, you should give the book a try, Holly! Or how about, you try this instead?" Mrs. Halley waved a copy of Jane Austin's *Pride and Prejudice* under Holly's snub nose.

After what seemed like hours, Mrs. Halley stopped forcing them reading books she brought with her.

"My eyes are drooping; and I need my beauty sleep so I can study for my exams!" complained Fay.

"Then let's light the fire, it's already seven!" Mrs. Halley gasped, looking at the time.

"First, let's set up our sleeping bags." Mr. Halley ordered.

Everyone set up their sleeping bags. Hazel took softest, warmest and cuddliest sleeping bag along with the softest pillow and heaviest blanket.

"Now, shall we light up our camp fire, now that everything else is ready?" Ava asked.

"Sure, I'll get the popcorn, marshmallows and some soup. I don't want bread balls in mine; not to forget when Bobby's grandma mixed chicken blood in it." Hazel laughed.

"Who's Bobby? When did you have chicken blood soup? You're a vegetarian." asked Fay.

"Bobby's my imaginary friend, you know. Bobby's just a friend I made up to entertain myself." Hazel lied; fibbing through her teeth.

"No time for cross talks, move those legs! Get the marshmallows, popcorn and soup!" interrupted Mrs. Halley.

"We'll collect the sticks," said the twins.

"And I'll set up the fire," Mr. Halley said with master flair in his confident voice.

Ava and Anna helped make the fire. They arranged the sticks and put stones around them. Mr. Halley dragged a few logs near the setting for seats.

"Oh no! I forgot the matches!" Mrs. Halley exclaimed.

"Don't worry, I'll rub two flints instead, and make a fire." Mr. Halley replied.

He rubbed the two stones and within minutes, there was a roaring fire.

"Come on! Grab a good seat by the fire." Mr. Halley called out.

"But first, grab a stick to warm up the marshmallow and Ava, do get a utensil to boil the soup in!" Mrs. Halley called out.

Hazel found a twisty rosewood stick. Holly found a stick made of holly. Ava found a short stick and Anna found a long one. They both were made of oak. Fay just continued to read.

Everyone sat down. Hazel and the twins, Holly and Mrs. Halley. Hazel looked at the fire's fiery flames rising. Red, orange and yellow were blended with gold as the fire flicked and merrily danced in the dark.

Mr. Halley absent-mindedly sat down. Instead of sitting on his seat, he sat on the fire itself!

"AAAAAAH!" he yelped. Mr. Halley, still whining like a puppy got up. It was like an electric shock for him to get up so quickly.

"HEEEEELP! MY PANTS ARE ON FIIIIIIREEEE!" Mr. Halley screamed, his pants still on fire and he could feel his blood curdle. He shrieked, his legs throbbing in pain.

"George!" Mrs. Halley screamed.

"What are you waiting for? Get the water right now! My pants are on fire!" Mr. Halley panicked.

The twins grabbed their water bottles and thew it all on the back of his pants. The fire burned a sizzling hole, right through it.

"Come dad, let's splash you with some more water, have some medicine and you can change, alright?" Ava said.

"Thanks dear," Mr. Halley whined, as Ava dragged him to her tent.

'Dad's so funny at times; he actually sat on a burning, flaming, flaring fire!' Hazel thought.

"What did I miss? I thought I heard dad screaming," said Fay, emerging from her tent, cool as a cucumber, calm as ever.

"Fay!" Hazel exclaimed in anger. It was so lame that dad's pants were on fire and here came Fay, asking what just happened.

Apparently, Mrs. Halley thought so too, and scolded, "Where have you been? I forbid you to read books in the holidays; so leave all your books right now!"

Hazel grinned smugly. Fay's jaw dropped, but she was scared of her mother right now. No arguing, or she would explode.

"Yes mummy," she soberly said, full of anger deep inside.

"Your dad's pants were on fire," she huffed.

"Is he okay?" asked Fay. Her mother nodded and Fay relaxed.

"I suppose we could have the marshmallows and soup tomorrow night. Who wants popcorn?" Hazel asked.

Nobody was in the mood for a meal after tonight's happenings. "I will!" Holly said, greedily munching the big bowl of buttery popcorn.

"Now my dears, let's get some sleep. Hazel, some special guests are coming tomorrow and we will spend the rest of our two weeks camping with them. I tried to make them come with us only, but unfortunately, they were busy. So, they're going to come tomorrow morning." Mrs. Halley smiled towards Hazel.

"Who is it?" she asked.

"You'll find out in the morning, Hazel my dear." Mrs. Halley grinned.

Suddenly, Mr. Halley came out with Ava. "I'm all better, ask no more when doc Ava and nurse Anna are there!"

"Daddy!" squealed Hazel, running towards him.

"Oh no!" Mrs. Halley said. "We don't have enough space for our guests!"

"Well, we must change our setting girls. Your mum and I can sleep in the kitchen tent, it's so big that I'm sure there'll be lots of space for us. The twins can sleep in their own tent with Holly. Fay and Annie will be fine; just the two of them... Hazel and her fri… oops! I mean the guests can sleep with her. We must change the setting now; we shall be sleeping by the time they arrive." Mr. Halley said.

"Alright then, we'll set up our sleeping bags in the kitchen tent then. Holly! Go in Anna and Ava's tent! It's good your dad ordered king-sized tents for us so that three people can easily sleep in one tent," ordered Mrs. Halley.

"How many guests are there altogether?" asked Hazel.

"Two," Mr. Halley swiftly replied.

'Who are these mystery guests?' Hazel asked herself, thinking. Surely, they couldn't be... could they? Sally, Lucy and Frank? No! There were two guests, not three.

Holly then sighed and dragged her sleeping bag to sleep in Ana and Ava's tent. Mr. and Mrs. Halley shifted their stuff in the kitchen tent.

Everyone boomed, "GOOD NIGHT!"

Then, they went in their cozy warm sleeping bags. "Aaah, this is soft," said Hazel, cuddling in her blanket.

Suddenly, she heard a whisper. "They should be here tomorrow."

Another voice said, "How did you call them?"

The first voice, which was a woman whispering, replied. “I found their numbers in Hazel’s drawer,” she said, carefully choosing what to reply.

“The decorations? Are they ready?” the second voice, which sounded like a man whispering.

“Honey dear, please relax! Her birthday is after a week, what will we do about the decorations right now?” fumed the voice of the woman.

“We better get some rest then; we want to be fresh when they come,” the man concluded.

“Night, sleep well,” the woman whispered.

And just then, snoring was heard.

“It sounded like mum and dad! Why should they fuss about my birthday right now? But I do have a good hunch who the guests are…” Hazel wickedly grinned.

Shutting her eyes, she too, fell asleep. It was very late. The owls hooted.

“Hazel, are you awake?” asked a timid voice.

“Ah!” gasped Hazel.

“Keep your voice down silly, it’s just us,” snapped another voice.

"Anna... Ava.... what are you doing here?" Hazel asked sleepily.

"We heard the Silly-Gilly-Gumball howling." Ava replied, scared.

"What's that?" Hazel inquired.

"Holly told us. A long time ago, this was a camping village with hundreds of houses. Then, the Silly-Gilly-Gumball, a creature with claws and fangs sharper than knives, bigger than a house, taller than a tree, with a tongue black as coal and purple skin, more purple than... um... purple... started haunting and patrolling the streets. He broke the houses and ate all the people. Legend is that you can hear its horrific howls at night too. In this place, there is a huge cave where the monster lives." Ava narrated her tale.

"I swear I heard it howl." Anna trembled.

"Urgh, babies! There are no Gumballs or whatever the monster's name is, Holly made up that tale to scare you. That 'howling' was the screeching of an owl, a screech owl," snarled Hazel. "Go back to your tent and I'll talk to mum!"

The twins left the tent. Angry and sleepy, stomping in her nightie, Hazel marched into her parents' tent.

"MOMMY!" she yelled. "Hazel! What is it? Go to sleep!" Mrs. Halley almost screamed.

"MUM! HOLLY IS NARRATING MONSTER TALES AGAIN AND THE TWINS CAME IN *MY* TENT, DISTURBING *MY* SLEEP, WAKING *ME* UP!" Hazel roared.

"That Holly, I'll give her a good whack. Scaring the girls like that. I'll deal with this situation, you go to bed, my dear." Mr. Halley said.

He marched up to Holly's tent. "Holly!" he yelled.

"Wah? Wath happened?" asked Holly, sleepily.

"I think you very well know, scaring the twins like that!" bellowed Mr. Halley.

"Sorry," said Holly.

"I'm warning you Holly, one more complaint, one more, and you're going home with Annie and Fay! They are also on my nerves! Fay, whining on her studies and Annie got twelve bug bites!" Mr. Halley said, trying to calm himself.

"Okay, night dad." Holly said, with a trace of fright in her voice. Mr. Halley left the tent that instant.

Hazel yawed and went back in her tent. Zzzzzzzzzzzzzzzzzzzz... peace at last.

CHAPTER FOUR

A LITTLE SURPRISE

The Sun rose up in the sky, the flowers merrily swayed with the breeze.

Hazel stirred as she heard a roaring engine. "Who is it?" she called out.

"Just hurry up, get dressed and come out of the tent!" came a voice.

Hazel work up with a start. She darted out of the tent and took a plunge in the icy cold stream.

Chatter, chatter, went her teeth. She was shivering. Quickly pulling on a yellow summer dress and a pair of slippers, she dried her hair. They looked curly.

Hazel was ready to greet the guests. They were standing behind her tent.

A girl with brown eyes and curly red hair folded her arms. She was wearing a frock like Hazel's, but it was white in colour.

The other girl standing next to her had tied her long blonde hair with a piece of red ribbon. She wore very old clothes, which were extremely filthy. Her top was loose and the pants were much too short for her. The girl wore some very dirty white sneakers too, Hazel had seen them before...

Hazel remembered that she had asked this girl why, but the girl refused to tell.

It was Hannah Hope and Rebecca Rose, her two best friends!

"What a pleasant surprise!" Hazel exclaimed, her heart fluttering with joy. "What are you doing here?" she further asked.

"Your mum called us, saying that she found our numbers in your drawer Hazel. She told us it's your birthday next week and we could come to celebrate, if we like. So we packed our bags and will stay with you till the time we are camping on the Seven Hills! SURPRISE!" squealed Rebecca.

"This is the best gift I could ask for!" exclaimed Hazel. "Come on! Let's have some fun!"

"What shall we do first?" Rebecca asked.

"Dig in the treats?" suggested Hannah.

"Not quite what I was thinking, we're grown up! Not babies like the twins!" scoffed Rebecca.

"Shall we go biking down the hills?" Hazel asked.

"A stroke of brilliance, I love biking!" commented Rebecca.

"And have a picnic too!" said Hannah.

"I shall leave a note where we are going," said Hazel, who was scared of her mum's reactions at times.

"I don't have a bike, my parents couldn't afford half of it," said Hannah, casually.

Hannah kicked herself for saying that. Her family wasn't rich. In fact, she feared that she would be made fun of and would lose her friends. It was her darkest secret and she forgot to guard her tongue again, and gave the game away.

"I guess you found out," sighed Hannah. "It's true that my parents aren't well off, which is why my stuff is second class. But even if we don't have a grand home, I love to spend the hols with them."

"I don't mind. I have met your parents. Your mother is the kindest darling on Earth." Rebecca said. "I'm having two younger siblings, who are twins. You'd love playing with Helix and Rhea, though Helix is quite the troublemaker."

"Sisters can be pests too," said Hazel, thinking about Holly and her abominable tricks. "Isn't Rhea one of Saturn's moons?" she further added.

"Yes, and Helix was named after Helix Nebula! I was named after a famous Space scientist. You see, most of our family is named after stars, nebulas, moons, scientists and galaxies, it's just tradition.

Though Harold Halley, the famous English astronomer is really not a bad choice of family heritage, Hazel. Ever wondered why your surname is Halley?"

"Don't be daft!" Hazel said.

Hazel could tell Hannah felt left out. She didn't have a grand family history.

"Hannah, come on, cheer up! Money and grandness isn't everything! Look at Millicent!

She's all grand and rich, but she's still a brainless git, isn't she?"

"I guess," stammered Hannah. "But can you keep that a secret? I worry that the others wouldn't like me anymore."

"Yeah, but how could they not like you, even if you tell them?" said Rebecca. "But nonetheless, I respect your decision. I won't tell them unless you want me to."

Hazel's friends were the best. How good it was to be a threesome again!

"Well then, let's build a tree house," said Hazel. "It'll be fun!"

"I can't climb a tree!" groaned Rebecca.

"You can get some milk, butter, bread, ham and eggs then," said Hannah, handing Rebecca a basket.

"From where?" asked Rebecca.

"From Ollie's Farm. I've heard that they have a litter of kittens you can adopt," drawled Hannah.

"I'll go then," giggled Rebecca and dashed off.

"Well then, let's make *our* tree house," snorted Hazel.

"Good riddance to bad rubbish, I mean, good riddance to bookworms." Hannah cringed.

They found a huge leafy oak tree which was perfect to make a tree house. It wasn't far from the campsite, so Mrs. Halley could keep an eye out for them.

Hannah gathered some rusty old wood and carved it with a chisel while Hazel tied the wooden boards with rope. She even made a pully system with the extra rope for Hannah to give the boards to Hazel easily.

Soon, they had a magnificent tree house with a swing made of rope and extra wood they had. Raiding Mrs. Halley's finest cushions, both the girls climbed the tree house.

"Well, I found something rather suspicious," hissed Hazel.

"An earthquake happened on the fourth hill and we had to set up camp here."

"Oh no!" gaped Hannah.

"Yes," continued Hazel. "I helped my family evacuate."

"I'm back!" cried Rebecca. Hazel and Hannah helped Rebecca climb the tree.

"Sorry about the food," shrugged Rebecca, pointing towards her empty basket. "But an earthquake on the second hill destroyed the farm, injured the cows and sheep, killed the chickens and kittens and Mrs. Dane, the lady who runs the farm is devastated. I helped clean the farm though."

"But why did the earthquake happen, that's all I want to know," said Hazel, gruffly.

"We'll soon find that out Hazel," assured Hannah.

"I hope so."

The time flew. It was Hazel's birthday. She wore her special birthday dress. It was a periwinkle blue dress with shiny pearls and pretty beading.

Hannah gave her a bright blue fountain pen covered in sparkly glitter.

Rebecca made a scrapbook with pictures of the trio and a few chocolates were stuck at the end.

Mrs. Halley made a cake and gave her some pocket money. Holly gave her sister a card. Fay, who was least bothered, gave an old book carelessly wrapped in brown paper.

The twins admired their sister and gave her a big bunch of lupins, lilacs, lavenders, daffodils, sunflowers, daisies, roses, dandelions and lilies(but no marigolds, as she didn't want to revive the memories of that idiot, Millicent Marigold).

Mr. Halley got Hazel a brand new lilac-coloured bike! It had a shiny silver bell, and fresh purple lavenders were neatly arranged in the basket.

"Let's take this bike for a ride! Hannah, you can have my old bike. It has some scratches, but totally fine. You can keep it," said Hazel.

Hannah's eyes twinkled. "Can I really keep your old bike?"

"Yes," grinned Hazel.

So the three friends rode their bikes after saying goodbye to Fay and Annie, who were going home.

"I guess we can sleep in Fay's tent, now," said Mrs. Halley.

"Who cares?" muttered Hazel.

Biking was fun. Hazel's new bike stood out. Rebecca's red bike was amazing, but she had a broken bell. Hannah slightly dented her new pink bike while falling over.

They raced across the plains. Hannah was a natural and managed to pull a few exquisite biking stunts. Her tire squeaked.

"Do you remember Millicent?" Hazel asked Rebecca.

"Never a dull moment without her. Pity her house is next to mine. She's got some new friends. I saw that conceited pig Lottie, and these new blokes for friends," groaned Rebecca.

"Who were they?" piped up Hannah.

"I heard their names. One was Grace Gracey, Ruby Red and the third was Stella. I didn't catch her last name though. Grace had silvery blonde hair and was um... graceful? Ruby had short red hair and freckles. Stella was tall, with large eyes and had golden curls." Rebecca replied, swiftly.

"Sounds like a bad lot," said Hazel, thoughtfully. "Yeah," agreed Hannah.

"Anyway, I had a row with Millicent. Instead of going to the park, I crashed in Millicent's garden party. It was too dark and I didn't have a torch." Rebecca laughed.

"Millicent would have been furious. It serves her jolly well right. What a beast of a girl she is!"

"Yeah, I can't wait to go back to school. I got a Wonkers's gift hamper for my birthday. Inside is a bumper trick which I shall play on the fox and her sidekicks. Millicent will have a scream," giggled Hannah. Everyone laughed. Hannah was a hoot.

Hazel and her friends had a blast. Talking, climbing trees, biking and swimming was fun. Holly wished she had such close friends.

The twins longed to go to Starway Academy and meet their true friends.

Soon, the worst days came. Packing. Screaming. Groaning. Mrs. Halley nosing in. Complete pandemonium. Distress. War zone. These were not very bad words to describe the event.

Mr. Halley loaded the luggage in the camper van. Hannah and Rebecca hogged up Fay's room. It was a really comfy journey.

"Pity all three of us can't be together in the same room," Hazel complained.

After a long drive and a few cries of the twins who wanted to stay, they finally reached home. Hannah's home was a cramped but tall place, like a jigsaw. Everything was untidy, and scattered.

STELLA

They arrived at Rebecca's house. It was on top of a hill. Hazel had the unpleasant surprise of having an encounter with Millicent Marigold, Lottie Little who was staying at her place and the three others Rebecca talked about.

Glaring at Millicent, she looked away. Can you guess what she was thinking? No? She was thinking of a suitable punishment for Millicent of course!

"Was that the Marigold in your form?" asked Holly.

"Yes," grunted Hazel. "Anyway, how do you tackle Snoddy? That's all I want to know because he's a bigger bully."

"That git? I get detention all the time from him. But a trick's worth playing on him!" giggled Holly. "However, Miss Pennywood is a tough nut to crack. I have to be sober in her lessons."

Sober? Sober was definitely *not* a word that described Holly Halley.

"Ooh, so that's how you didn't make a mayhem this family camp. You're getting sensible like me. But don't go all goody-goody," said Hazel.

"As if I would!" laughed Holly.

"Did you play any tricks last year?" asked Hazel.

"Some of them. Not good ones. Don't have a partner yet. But I will now. Hilda from my old day school will come to our school this year. And so will Henna," said Holly.

Finally they were home. Holly and Hazel raced in the house and went inside.

After a mouth-watering dinner of rolls, potted meat, salad and crispy crunch waffles, Hazel lay exhausted in her room.

"Wow, that really was the worst trip ever, but it was fun nonetheless." Hazel said to herself. "I'm glad to be home."

CHAPTER FIVE

BACK TO STARWAY ACADEMY

This time, only Mr. and Mrs. Halley went to Starway Street to get Hazel, Holly and Fay's school books and things.

To pass the time, she studied her school books. Hazel loved flipping through the pages of her Aliens book. It was full of colours and pictures of funny creatures. Fay was delighted.

"Today's the day!" cried Hazel.

"Sunday," replied Holly.

"No, you idiot. We're going to Starway Academy again," smiled Hazel.

"We'll be going next year too!" squealed Ava.

"You'll be babies! I'll be in the fourth form and Hazel will be in the third form. And Fay in the sixth!" scoffed Holly.

"Oh yeah," Anna slumped in defeat. She wanted to show Hazel everything in her new school and the friends she would make. The twins totally forgot that Hazel would be a mighty third-former by then.

"Don't worry," said Hazel, looking at Ava's woebegone face. "I'd love to meet your friends.

"Really?" Ava asked.

"Totally!" Hazel replied.

"Cool beans."

Hazel was fond of the twins and had long nursed a soft corner for them.

"Here we are," Holly cried as she saw a midnight blue bus with eight floors.

"Don't forget Polly!" reminded Mrs. Halley. And then, she gave Hazel a kiss. Holly sniggered until she got her kiss.

Dashing for Polly's cage, Hazel clambered aboard. Polly was her beautiful emerald green parrot and was like a friend.

She searched the compartments for her friends.

In the last compartment was Henry, Tom, Hannah and Rebecca!

"Oh Hazel! How are you?" asked Hannah, giving her a hug.

"Fine," mumbled Hazel. "I couldn't find you anywhere."

"How's Ginny and Tibbles?" asked Hazel.

"The furball is gaining weight," said Hannah, pointing towards her guinea pig.

"And Tibbles is as happy as ever." Rebecca told.

"So, Polly's here too." Hannah said.

"Yeah," replied Hazel and Polly chirped.

"Oh, we're sorry Hazel, but the compartment is full!" squeaked Rebecca.

"Oh," sighed Hazel. "Who are the other two?"

"You know Charles? The one with shiny black hair, grey eyes and pinkish cheeks?" asked Hannah.

"Yeah," said Hazel.

"Henry is his best friend," Hannah stated, pointing towards a chilled-out, fun-looking boy.

His hair were done in a messy quiff, and he had a comical nose.

"And Tom here, he's the third one in their group." Rebecca said.

"Hello Hazel," said Tom. He was tall, clever and had dark hair. His eyes were striking, emerald green in colour and he had long white fingers. Hazel thought he was decent and a brainiac. Books. He was a perfect friend for Rebecca, as books were her life.

Hannah was more of the sporty types, so naturally, Hazel expected her to get along with Henry more.

"I suppose we'll get going then," muttered Tom and went out of the compartment along with Henry. "We'll find Charles, you can sit with your friends."

They found Charles and sat in another compartment together.

Hazel sat down with her friends and as usual, they had a blast. They didn't sleep all night and talked about things at home and a little about the adventure last year.

All the students came out of the bus, chattering.

CHARLES AND HENRY

"Snoddy will do a bunk this year. He expected that fail the exam and be expelled!" said Hannah. Everyone giggled.

The grounds were vast. Bees were buzzing in and out of the pennyroyal. The Surfing Sea was aqua blue in colour.

Proudly pinning her silver Surfwink badge, she went inside the Great Hall.

"Look at the five," Hannah viciously hissed. Millicent and Lottie sat down together, their cold eyes so alike.

Ruby rubbed her freckled nose as she plaited Stella's golden tresses. Grace sat there, looking eerie with her silvery blonde hair. She might have been a porcelain figure, and easily the best ballerina in the school.

"This supper is scrumptious," remarked Rebecca, nearly swallowing her chicken.

"I agree," nodded Hazel.

"Can I just *look* at that badge?" asked Hannah gazing longingly at the Catcher badge gleaming proudly on her chest.

"Sure," replied Hazel, bursting with pride. Many others stared at her badge; Hazel made herself *quite* popular.

Millicent and her gang looked enviously. "She has a Star Lighter, just look at it. All I have is Drifting Dragon." Lottie moaned.

"I have a Slithering Serpent." Millicent said, haughtily.

"But even the Serpent is rubbish compared to her board!" remarked Stella.

"What do you have then, a Crashing Comet for a Drift Board?" snapped Millicent.

Stella looked as if she might explode, because she *did* have a Crashing Comet.

"Cheer up, I have a Turbo Twenty-Two Thousand. I can share." Ruby offered as Stella nodded.

"At least my Fanged Flier is better than Hannah's Slow Sloth." Grace chirped.

Hannah had a third-class Slow Sloth board. Some of the crow feathers had fallen so she couldn't keep it in the air for a long time. The grey polish was coming off. There were some dents in the wood and sharp edges as well.

"I got the Twisting Tail-Turner this year, so you can have my Bolt Blaster 600. It has some paint peeling off but it is fast and can fly high. You can paint it and it will look amazing." Rebecca said.

"I'm tired of using old stuff. I wish I could have something new for a change but I'm in no position to. Gee, thanks Sniffles." Hannah grinned.

Millicent marched off with her tiny nose stuck in the air, so jealous she could practically explode.

Lottie rushed off with her like a puppy. Grace glided forward. Stella gazed and went off with Ruby, furious at Millicent's Crashing Comet comment.

Hazel too, got ready to leave and look at the dormitory.

The dormitory was pretty much the same, with the spacious common room. Unfortunately, Millicent chose the bed next to Rebecca!

"Oh Lottie! I got the perfect place to spy on them. I shall know what tricks they will play on me!" she said.

"And we can spy on her too!" huffed Hazel. "She forgot that bit, didn't she?"

The next day was perfect to play Surfwink.

Alicia was the captain. She had short blonde hair and a determined gaze. Kelly and Terry were the Snatchers. Alicia was the Defender while Hazel, Katie Blue and Amy Benson were the Catchers.

"This board is the all-time keeper and is the best board here, Hazel. I have a Roaring Thunder which is quite fast. Oh nice! I like the Thunderbolt Kelly. Very agile, swift and supple." Alicia commented.

"Don't show me that scandalized White Rabbit, we'd be laughed at, Katie. And Terry, your Green Gator is dreadful!"

"My father has ordered a Galloping Glider, it'll come tomorrow by post!" said Terry, indignantly.

"Ah, I can order a Lightning Lion for you Katie!" said Alicia.

"Alright," grinned Katie, cheerfully.

"Well Amy, you have a Racing Rainbow. Cool!" commented Alicia.

After that, Hazel was handed a midnight blue bag. It had a slinky swim suit and a writing pad for Surfwink matches, timetables and notes.

The word 'Starway Academy' was emblazoned in gold letters on her bag, swimsuit and the writing pad.

"Your gear," said Alicia, tartly. Then, she waved her hand as Pop the porter brought a huge board with complicated diagrams.

"Now, copy this stuff," instructed Alicia.

Hazel used her Extra-Quick Quill to write. Within a minute, she said, "I'm done!"

The rest took a few more minutes to copy. Alicia wasn't pleased with them.

"Let me explain this stuff," said Alicia. "Part one of my plan. Amy, you catch the ring that is far from the unicorn. The opponents will rush towards you and you shall distract them. Hazel, you catch a ring near the unicorn. Katie, block the Defender. Hazel would have a clear shot."

She explained her entire chart. After they were excused to go. "Oh, and one more thing. This isn't a session. Just an introduction. We'll waste no time doddling like dodos."

After the exhausting training session that followed, she went to have some supper. Hannah and Rebecca were waiting for her. The three went inside the main building together, and had an unpleasant encounter with Millicent Marigold.

"Hello Millicent," said Rebecca, wryly. Hannah eyed her with deepest loathing.

"Ah! The ice block has come! Can't speak? Blue in the face? A blue baboon? BOO!" Millicent teased.

"Too bad you didn't. It would have been a scream to see Lottie burst into tears and squeal like a pig." Hazel retorted.

"Come on, girls." Hannah said and dragged Hazel away.

"Let's sit in the garden, then." Rebecca said.

"Yes, now that Hazel stopped the comet, we can go out again!" squealed Hannah.

"One day, can I meet the Blobs too?" asked Rebecca.

"They're weird things. But funny and cute. Tiny Tinky was adorable." Hazel said.

Just then, the bell rang. RIIIIIING!

"Time for class," said Rebecca, cheerfully. "We got some new subjects this year."

"Which ones?" asked Hannah, scratching her head with confusion. She hunted for her missing timetable, but had no luck.

Hazel checked her new timetable before saying, "According to this waste of a paper, it's Star Gazing and Formation, whatever that is."

First period was Reflections. Snoddy was in a particularly vindictive mood. Hannah wasn't expelled as he hoped.

"Today," he said, snarling, "We will create something in pairs. Today, we shall create the reflection which comprises of three ingredients only. I want you all to make it right now. Let idea's flow and bubble in your so stupid minds. Enjoy the silence. Now let me see, who shall be your partner, Hope?"

CHAPTER SIX

A TROUBLESOME TIME

"Ah yes," he grinned wickedly, bouncing across the room. "You and Miss Millicent. Halley and Rose. Louella and Gracey. "

And so on…

He dug his hands in the large pockets of his trench coat and gave Hazel a cold stare with his icy eyes.

Hazel looked back boldly, not afraid. She glared at him as Rebecca created a mixture of Fusion powder and Crystallizer.

They covered it with some foil and waited for the solution to cool.

Aliens was a lot better. They learned about Noxes, dark creatures which drained light and

MISS PENNYWOOD

warmth. They were like mossy boulders with rotting skin and eight red eyes.

Professor Potts spoke in a strange high-pitched squeak. His face was pale and peaky. That was because he had been the comet's victim.

But still the flicker of joy in his eyes never died and the flame was still dancing inside.

Space Science was as hard as ever. Diagrams, rulers, Maths, the classical. "Does Jupiter make an angle with Saturn at this position?" asked Hazel.

"Hmmm… It's Uranus that aligns with Saturn at this point of time," replied Miss Pennywood, brushing her golden tresses aside. Hazel looked down at her chart. Her diagram was all wrong!

Everyone was excited for Space Gardening. "This is a carnivorous plant, the Moon Weed." Miss Linnie said.

It looked as if she had spent all morning preparing for this lesson. Her curly grey locks and green dress was caked with mud and a bunch of other... slimy, worm-like creepy crawlies Hazel preferred not to name.

"Who knows what they are?" she asked.

Rebecca confidently replied, "Moon Weed is a thorny black plant with no leaves, only pearly white flowers. Teeth, which are sharp as knives grow on the petals. It grows in the doomy darkness and it eats insects. Its fleshy stem contains a rare, powerful substance which works only on a full Moon night."

"Er... Yes! And I shall teach you how to handle these weeds as Miss Rose so rightly said." Miss Linnie said.

Nobody except Hannah could collect a drop of that powerful pus. It was useless as it wasn't the full Moon, but just to practice. The razor-sharp thorns created deep cuts and gnashes on their hands.

Hannah, who was beaming, proudly presented a bottle of the pus to Miss Linnie. Surprisingly, she didn't hurt herself at all!

"You just have to tickle their petals. And the thorns will sort of vanish." Hannah said.

There were only four lessons as it was the first day back. Within a few hours, Hazel completed the vast amount of homework she was given.

"I'm tired," she groaned.

"Let me look at your essay, I've got to write sixteen more inches to complete Potts's five feet essay."

"Do your own work!" snapped Rebecca, who was rather touchy about studies. She had already finished, while Hazel was on the verge of completing it.

Hazel frowned and the scratching of her quill stopped. She examined her last few paragraphs more carefully and splotches of ink glittered on the parchment.

"No, that's not right," she said as she crumpled it and dived for a copy of *Nocturnal Aliens and their Facts*.

Hannah grabbed the crumpled parchment that Hazel had thrown on the floor and skimmed through it. "Brilliant!" she said and began to copy it down in her big loopy writing.

"Thanks Tufty, you bailed me out of this one! You see, my handwriting's larger than yours, so it'll help fill up the parchment. Professor didn't specify the word limit, did he now?" Hannah added.

Hazel thought it was a brilliant loophole, but clearly, Rebecca didn't agree. She snorted disapprovingly through pursed lips. Her mouth became thin and she completed another composition for Snoddy.

They next day, it was no surprise to find that the solution Hazel and Rebecca had left to cool was flaming hot. It was obvious that Snoddy had tampered with it.

Rebecca furiously gnashed her teeth, tinkered with the ingredients and left it there to cool. Again. After fifteen minutes, she stirred it till it was a clear crystal blue.

Hazel scooped some of it in a flask, put the cork on and sealed it with wax so Snoddy could not ruin it, again!

"Ooh, I'm excited! We have Space Gardening and Star Gazing tonight at eight!" squealed Rebecca.

But Space Gardening was in for an unfortunate twist. Miss Linnie caught a cold, and Miss Pennywood was substituting for her.

It was clear that she had never been in a garden before, and by the end of the class, the class burst into hysterical giggles.

The prim and proper Miss Pennywood who gave detention to anyone even with a drop of mud anywhere on their clothes, herself looked like a giant mudball.

Hannah said as tears of laughter rolled down her eyes, "Oh my, that's the best laugh I had in ages. Miss Pennywood looks as if she mud wrestled a very large, smelly pig!"

Rebecca hiccoughed down her laughs, kept a stern expression and said, "If I knew this class was going to be more of a circus, then I wouldn't have come."

She was a good laugh, but she was a bit too serious and irritated at the slightest mistake in class.

Hazel stared blankly and then, laughed harder. "My ribs hurt now; I could have died when I saw her examining the popping Mudbubble Buttercups. I swear Miss Linnie rigged them herself! The moment when the Buttercups splashed mud on her face was hysterical."

"Star Gazing will be better," huffed Rebecca. "I know it will."

"Let's go to Star Gazing now," said Hazel and went up to the Tremendous Telescope.

It was tremendous (duh, it was called the Tremendous Telescope for a reason). It had a shiny coat of midnight blue and stood on small tires.

Miss Primsoll, their teacher was fragile like a porcelain figure. It seemed as if you knocked her over, she would smash to pieces. Her crimpy brown hair were piled up on her head like an updo.

She was not a day older than twenty and wore a tight-fitted emerald dress. A rhinestone-studded shawl was perfectly draped around her pretty neck.

Through that mammoth telescope, they could see stars, planets and galaxies up close.

The sky was full of jewels that glittered like diamonds. It was like a roof, the most beautiful one.

"Hello dears," she said in a misty voice. "I'm Miss Primsoll, and I'll teach you Star Gazing."

Hazel giggled, and she wasn't the only one. What kind of name was Primsoll? It kind of sounded like the plimsolls she wore on weekends.

"Now, let's begin. We shall observe Proxima Centauri today. It's unusually bright. Please write a composition about the gas fuelling the stars and their properties. Two feet. Take out your quills everyone!"

Hazel groaned as referred to the gas names and properties interpreting *A Guide to Gases*.

A part of their project was to draw a Star Chart and the matter and material they release into the universe to create smaller stars. They were to be written in key points.

Space Science was extra hard the next day. Miss Pennywood wanted everyone to write another long composition. She even presented a task which would be 'fun'.

They had to do some complicated sums which involved measurement and scaling. The 'fun' part of the so called 'task' was that they had to make a map of the planetary system and record everything in it, even the moons of Jupiter, with scaling and precise measurements.

After that was Formations. Professor Fint was the Formations teacher. He was a tiny man who was hardly four-feet tall and his small eyes were just visible under his round glasses.

"Hello my students. Today is the day for..." Professor Fint squeaked.

Just then a woman entered. She had her blonde hair set up elaborately in curls, red on her cheeks and wore a foul, sap green dress.

"I'm Charity Mint," she said. "If you don't mind me asking, where did you get that disgraceful coat? Never mind, we must get this interview started. I have so many questions; I don't know where to start!"

Millicent sniggered.

"I need this for my broadcasting channel. And I need the juicy stuff!" Charity continued as she wrinkled her nose.

The class sat silently and Charity beamed. She asked a few questions for Professor Fint to answer about their coursework and lessons. He tried his best to speak calmly, but he was shaking with anger.

"Thank you," said Charity and swept away.

"As I was saying…" continued Professor Fint now that Charity had gone.

Meanwhile, Charity's interview with Professor Fint was the big bold news today. She edited and changed everything to the point that she had twisted his name.

"Professor 'Flint', has recently agreed to take up on the post of Formations at Starway Academy.

Marool Morag stated, "He is so tiny that I can't spot him at all. It was quite comical in class to hear his terrified sort of squeak. It's difficult to hear him and understand what he is saying."

Gabriola Gracey said, "He is scared of the Headmistress, Miss Pennywood. Honestly, he was shivering and hiding behind his own desk!"

"Should a teacher like that be allowed to teach? Should this kind of staff be hired to teach and hone the young, impressionable minds of the students? Miss Pennywood ought to take charge of this situation! Till then, stay tuned!"

Charity concluded with a simpering note in her voice. That lady was pure trouble who only wanted to destroy people's reputation and throw it in the gutter for her own selfish reasons.

Hazel wanted to get some dirt on Charity, so that she could realise how others felt when she said mean things about them.

As she sat in the common room, trying to think of a way to outwit Charity, Hannah marched with a smile on her face.

"Well, I saw a poster today." Hannah announced, her eyes sparkling.

"What did you see?" shrieked the class.

"I shouldn't know this, but we will celebrate Hallowe'en this year with a party. I saw a flyer sticking out of Miss Pennywood's door. I grabbed it and made a run for it. So, we've got a month or more with us, I'm not good at Maths."

Everyone cheered.

Millicent was conversing with Bibbly Bikkins, who looked like a pug or a ferocious bull terrier.

In other words, he was just as ugly and awful as Millicent was. Hazel had to laugh at that.

Ugly, snorty giggles.

What a pair they were!

CHAPTER SEVEN

HALLOWE'EN

Charity was buzzing around school and asking random students for news. She popped in between lessons and collected interviews.

She wrote it all down and blabbed it all in her broadcasting channel, the Daily News.

But as Charity lapped up all the news, she put in major twists and the person didn't come out looking too good.

When Miss Pennywood flatly refused to give an interview, Charity described her as a moody, bad-tempered flamingo.

It was partially true, since Miss Pennwyood was a little bad-tempered, if Hazel was honest with herself, but how dare Charity describe her that way for all the world to hear!

After that, Charity was forbidden to come inside the school, but used the trips to Starmade as her advantage.

When the students went to the little village, she pestered them give more whereabouts of the school.

Today, the radio was on. Charity spoke in her girlish giggle.

"Hazel Halley – a daring hero or a tattling trickster?

Hazel Halley, a girl of eleven claims to have saved the students in the school of Starway Academy from being frozen. Mysteriously, many of them had turned into blocks of ice.

Rumour has it that she rode the legendary Comet of Ice into Space and destroyed it all on her own. The details of this adventure will be in the front page of the paper tomorrow."

But is this true?

"Halley is a pathetic fake. Who knows? She might have said that to grab attention. Maybe, she cooked up this cock and bull story to be in the spotlight as usual," stated Millicent Marigold, a sincere student.

"I think she's worthy to be investigated and evidence is yet to be revealed. Without proof, I conclude that this is a lie," added the charming Lottie Little.

"So friends, keep watching the Daily News for more informative information, hot off the press."

Hazel walked up to Millicent and made eye contact. Her face was red and she was about to burst like a bomb.

"Ah!" sniggered Millicent. "Here comes the popular tattletale. What's up Halley? What's your next interview about?"

Just then, Hazel punched Millicent right in the face! Her silly smile was wiped off as she whimpered.

"Little coward," sneered Hazel, spitefully, watching Millicent sob. "That'll teach her a lesson."

From that day, things were peaceful. Hallowe'en was round the corner and so, everybody went shopping for dresses in Starmade.

Rebecca was drooling over a turquoise blue gown made of blue satin. It was a light and breezy dress and it would look simply stunning.

Rebecca pooled in her gems and she also bought a pretty blue rose to put on her hair.

Hannah gazed longingly at a pretty gold-sequined dress, but staring at the price tag made her throw up. So, she wandered towards the other dresses on the snotty-looking mannequins.

Hazel went to Dresses of Dreams and instantly found her dress.

It was a pretty pale pink, and like a flowing evening gown. There was no design on the fabric, but it was made of stunning satin, and had a bow on the waist.

She gaped and instantly asked the shopkeeper for the dress the moment she set her eyes on it.

"Five greens, two purples if you please," said a woman with stubby fingers and a face like a cat. The dress was certainly ravishing, and Hazel instantly handed in the gems.

Hazel squealed in delight as she showed her friends her dress. Hannah gave a weak little smile and said, "Nice, I hope I look that pretty, or even close to that." Rebecca beamed and admired her dress.

"Is it your tablecloth? What is that ugly thing?" laughed Millicent.

Hazel retorted, "Have you seen yourself in the mirror? You're as ugly as a toad yourself!"

Not wishing to fight with Hazel, she picked upon Hannah. "And what have you got? A dishrag, Hope? Surely," she cackled.

"Ooh, I'll get her for this, she struts all over the place." Hannah said. Rebecca nodded as the three went back to the academy.

"Do show your dress, Hannah, oh please..." begged Rebecca.

"Fine," said Hannah, gloomily. "Just don't laugh."

"Alright," said Hazel, bracingly. "Just show the dress."

Hannah's dress wasn't that bad as Hazel thought it would be. True, it was second hand, but then it was pretty.

The minty green dress was so casually elegant with only a few seams done on it. The gauzy organza billowed with the breeze.

There were three patches and there were a few splotches of gravy on the sleeves. However, it was a pleasant effect altogether.

They went back the school. The trees changed their clothes from green to red and gold. The fallen leaves were bundled up in piles.

They had shining gold skin, and were paper thin. One fell on Hazel's head, landing on a leafy bed. There were masses of yellow, orange and red on the ground, with the scent of autumn all around!

***

After a few days, Hallowe'en had arrived.

Hazel looked at herself in the mirror as she twirled in her dress. She also put some Springtime Hair Cream to make her hair sleek and shiny, and it was twisted into a knot.

Jack 'o' lanterns were surrounding the school and placed all around the boundaries. Cobwebs made of string were spread across the school.

Plastic bats and spiders hung from the roof. The lights were off and little lights were floating across the room. The Great Hall was decorated with orange and black streamers.

But the Great Hall was easily the most beautifully decorated room. It was so huge that the entire school could be seated comfortably.

Lessons were dismissed that day. Everyone was there to party.

Hannah looked thoroughly embarrassed when the other girls who wore every colour of the rainbow, teased her relentlessly. But, in Hazel's opinion, she looked 'cool'.

Rebecca was the 'Girl in Blue' and the blue rose looked pretty indeed.

Millicent looked murderous when she saw Hazel. She herself looked like an ugly sasquatch in that hideous bottle green dress with long gloves.

Lottie wore a drab grey which complimented her mousey hair. Grace wore a silver gown which emitted a pearly glow. She was slender, tall and graceful.

Stella twirled her gold tresses as she swayed in lacy, frilly pink dress.

Ruby wore the stunning gold dress Hannah really wanted. Even she looked pretty in that.

Charles looked like some sort of annoying duke in his black tuxedo and bowtie, while Henry looked like a clown(though very much expected from him). His socks were inside out, his sleeves were rolled up and his tie was totally lopsided.

Hannah and Henry filled their plates with snacks as they battled over who could make the funniest pizza.

Tom was decked out in grey and he sat by the snack table with Rebecca, rambling about schoolwork.

Roland, Larry, Terry, Greg, Adam, Julian, Edward and the other hundreds of boys were sitting on the 'boys only' table and chattering.

The girls loved hanging around like a pack of wolves. Bridget, Katie, Alicia, Bonnet, Susan, Marybelle, Juliet, Leah and the other girls smiled and batted their eyelashes like professionals.

The snack table was everyone's favourite. Many students sat there. The meals were creatively designed.

Creepy Cookies in the shape of ghosts, Pumpkin Pizza that had a pumpkin on it, made with various toppings like peppers, carrots, olives and cheese. Spooky Spaghetti with red meatballs were served. The blood red meatballs made it look really spooky.

Ghost goodies, which were just Hallowe'en candy, tasted like gumdrops and melted snickerdoodles. Many more meals with way more bizarre names were aligned neatly across the vast table.

On a much smaller table, chocolate milk, fruity juice and Hawaiian punch were lavishly set up and arranged.

Hazel piled up some Creepy Cookies and the chocolate milk on her plate. Hazelnut crunches were buried like treasure in the cookies.

The chocolate milk was cool and refreshing. She sipped through it with the paper straw.

Charles was sipping his smoothie. He put it on the counter and smiled. "Ah!" he said. "So, there you are."

"It's hot, isn't it?" he said, fanning himself with Henry's tie.

"Oy!" Henry said. Charles mumbled an apology.

"I agree. Letting my hair down is so not my style." Hazel replied, wrinkling her nose, eyeing her neat hair in distaste. She far preferred her carefree look.

Hannah was staring at them, nodding her head as if to say 'come over'.

"Can I just use the restroom?" fibbed Hazel.

"Sure, I'll see you in a bit." Charles replied.

Charles sat down on a bench. Hazel joined her friends.

Fay was nearby. "Why aren't you wearing a dress?" asked Hazel, innocently.

"Dress, what dress?" asked Fay.

"It's Hallowe'en! We all wear dresses!"

"I thought it was a special session for the International Exchange!" gaped Fay.

"Yeah, well, try getting a calendar next time to keep track of your events." Hazel smirked and left.

Rebecca held Tibbles, her little kitten in her arms. She purred loudly as she snuggled against her silky dress.

Hazel laughed.

"Hazel! Just look at that chocolate fountain! Come on!" Hannah moaned with longing.

"Let's go then!" Hazel agreed.

Out of the corner of her eye she saw Tom. He stood there with Rebecca, examining Tibbles with bright interest, but his expression remained blank.

Bibbly Bikkins had a coy smile on his face as he gossiped with his gang. They all were ugly ducklings and rude to everyone.

Marool Morag, Roger Kole, Kelvin Cody, Millicent, Stella, Ruby, Grace and Lottie were chatting like there was no tomorrow.

Meanwhile, they had fun for a few hours, Rebecca was an amazing dancer.

After that, a little growl was heard. It grew louder and louder.

Just then, it rained cats and dogs. Rain poured through the ceiling. The aggressive clouds roared like Mrs. Halley did when she was angry.

The odd part was that a second ago the night was perfectly clear and cloudless; Miss Primsoll had been stargazing.

Everyone was shocked. But Rebecca said, "Honestly, aren't you two dummies? Some problem is occurring as its impossible that one moment the sky is clear and the next moment, the clouds are on a roll."

Hazel piped up, "Yeah but let's go before the thunder st…"

BANG! CRASH! BOOM! THUNDER STRUCK!

The forks of lightning were terrifying. Next, there was a click as all the lights went off. So did the little lights in their air. The music stopped. Everything was pitch black.

Miss Pennywood lit up a candle. Students were handed torches. "Using these," said the Headmistress, pausing for breath. "Please go back to your dormitories and change your dresses, QUICKLY!"

Everyone scattered. The torches were powerful enough to lead Hazel to her closet.

Hannah was feeding dinner to Ginny and Rebecca was straining herself to read one last book before bed.

After that Miss Pennywood gravely announced that it was time for bed.

Everyone was muttering about the party.

"I wish it could have lasted longer!"

"Yeah, but I bet Halley's happy. Urgh, why waste such a lovely pink dress on sly foxes like her?"

"Who cares?"

Just then, the dormy door creaked open. The five squealed and jumped to their beds.

A prefect said in his deep assuring voice, "Is everything okay girls?"

"Yes!" giggled Lottie. "I'll continue my patrol then," said Harry and walked away.

CHAPTER EIGHT

CHARMWOOD CHAMPIONS VS STARWAY ACADEMY

The merciless weather was getting colder as the fall ended and the first Surfwink match was starting within a week.

Alicia kept their mouths to grindstone. Amy Benson was getting on with Hazel very well. She had dreadlocks and eyes dark as an expresso coffee.

Hazel was so tired. Miss Pennywood gave a droning lecture about the distance between the centre of the Milky Way's black hole and Earth.

Snoddy wanted them to create a difficult fiddly solution for Reflections.

Even Professor Potts wanted them to write an essay on Aliens.

Miss Primsoll forced them to write a composition about Arcturus, a star that Hazel and Hannah were clueless about.

Hazel barely had time to plot or chatter with her friends.

They had a training practice with the Charmwood Champions who had come for the match and slept in the Rumbling Ruins for a few days, creating beds with rugs, flax or heather.

Charmwood Academy was the real name of the school, but they named their Surfwink team as Charmwood Champions.

Alicia warned them not to use their best moves until the match, because the opponents could use their own moves against them.

And that is when Hazel saw the unicorn foal. It was simply beautiful with white skin and a shining gold mane and tail. Its bright eyes twinkled as it examined Hazel, prancing.

Then, it neighed and spread out it's beautiful white wings and playfully flew off.

"This is the unicorn foal we'll play with tomorrow. We use them instead of adults because they are a lot faster," explained Alicia.

And then, the practice game began. Hazel peered in to catch on of the rings. She sped towards it, but was blocked by a Snatcher.

Amy caught the first ring and tossed it, but missed.

There were many misses and goals. The rings seemed to multiply by the dozen. The pink and blue blurs were hard to see, and the foal kept changing into a sea-unicorn, which was aggravating, but made the game much more thrilling and exciting for spectators.

It's hind legs vanished, and was replaced with a silvery fish tail with glittering scales! It went down the water, leapt back in seconds, and was a normal unicorn again. And then, it spread its wings and flew off!

Starway Academy narrowly beat Charmwood Champions. Alicia flooded with tears and announced that they were to practice harder, and fled from the stadium.

Hazel gulped. The match was going to be terrifying!

The next day came. She changed into her midnight blue costume and the Charmwood Champions arrived, dressed in canary yellow uniforms.

Madam Melinda blew the whistle and turned the hourglass. Hazel squeaked with fright but replaced her look with a bold grimace.

The crowd cheered. It seemed as if the whole school had come. All of them wore midnight blue shirts and cheered her on.

However, Millicent, Lottie, Ruby, Stella, Grace and a few others wore a sunny yellow. They booed Hazel, but she didn't mind.

Katie, Amy and Hazel grinned at each other. They were ready.

"And off they go!" screeched the magical microphone. "It's Halley streaking down, surfing- oh dear, a high wave is coming up- will she- yes she passed it- flying up- oh I say, SHE CAUGHT A RING!"

The crowd yelled out their praise. Just then, a Snatcher tripped Hazel of her board and the ring broke free from her grip.

"FOUL!" screamed the microphone. She was dangling off her board. With her reflexes born in training, she swung and caught the ring again with her foot!

Flipping back on the board, she dashed and plunged towards the water. Amy and Katie blocked the Snatchers and Hazel accelerated, speeding up like a bullet, flipping on the back on her board, she threw the ring with all her might, but the unicorn flew away!

She chased it and finally, with the ring in her hand, she aimed for its horn. The Defender, taken by surprise, didn't catch it at all. Hazel scored!

The microphone continued, "And after that tremendous effort from Halley- John March of the Charmwood Champions grabs another ring and dashes towards the foal- Alicia the Defender dives after and swims in the water!"

Catching the ring, Alicia was red with pleasure as she passed it to Katie. A snatcher flew towards her, but Katie passed the ring to Amy, Amy passed the ring to Hazel and passed it back to Katie.

"That's it! Blue and Frost pass it on- and Blue scores!" the microphone further commented.

The Charmwood Champions were disheartened. Their spirit was crushed.

Again and again they scored, defended all the rings and the captain of Charmwood Champions, Quigsley Quirk, pulled his sleek white blonde hair.

With ease, Starway Academy won, won the first match with three ninety points to twenty!

And then, Madam Melinda shared the score of the first match between all four schools.

Starway Academy was first, Charmwood Academy was second. The other two schools, the Knightly Educational Institute of Night and Dr. Sprocket's School of Space were third and fourth.

Hazel smiled triumphantly and Alicia sobbed hard into her face, too proud for words. Amy and Katie hugged each other, while Kelly and Terry beamed with pleasure.

Quigsley was screaming at John, who was angry because of his embarrassing defeat. All of the team we in tears and looked extremely woebegone.

The crowd meanwhile, went wild and roared with thunder. They got up, shrieking their heads off, stamping and jumping and cheering like a bunch of wild animals.

Snoddy bared his teeth at Hazel, but she was pleased. All the teachers looked cheerful, and the sober Miss Pennywood stood with pride.

Hazel had a daydream of winning the Surfwink Cup as well. Everybody would be off the charts, and that made her laugh.

But then, she blinked and looked dignified. She must work harder at Surfwink and of course, write to her family.

Mrs. Halley posted a short, but flattering letter to her, which made Hazel strut around the common room.

She was tired of hearing the endless comments of praise, as she saw Millicent scowl and hugged her friends tightly.

While she might want a bit of attention now and then, but this wasn't it. She didn't want the glory, not in that way. All this praise made her feel sick.

Still, she read her mother's letter with a smile on her face.

Dear Hazel,

We all are so, so proud of you! I knew that you had it in you, your father was an excellent Catcher in his days. I threw a party, and baked chocolate truffle cream cake, glazed with chocolate, just the way you like it! Share it all with your friends and remember that daddy and I miss you so much! We hope that you enjoy your treat and have a great time at school. Give my love to you and your friends as well. I shall, of course, write next week, dear. See you soon!

Love

Mom(and Dad)

Hazel clutched the letter and ripped the square parcel wrapped in brown paper.

True to her word, Mrs. Halley had baked an enormous chocolate cake with sprinkles.

She cut herself a slice and munched greedily on it. Nibbling it with relish, she smacked her lips and cut herself another slice.

More than half of the cake was left, and so, she divided it into four pieces.

Two for Hannah, who loved chocolate almost as much as she did, a small piece for Rebecca who preferred strawberry swirl, and the last slice for Holly.

"You showed the Charmwood Champions and everyone else that you're an incredible player. No one will dare mess with you now, not even Millicent!" giggled Hannah. Rebecca congratulated Hazel as well.

"Group hug!" cried Amy and Katie, entering the common room.

And the five hugged each other tightly and squealed.

Of course, the next match was against the other two schools, and so, Starway Academy would wait for a while to play the next match.

Everyone was congratulating Hazel except for Millicent, who was loudly whining about 'politics' and 'cheating'. She had a quarrel with Hazel and the entire dormitory was soon at war.

And so the fight went on... No one noticed the clouds rage… or the blinding flash of light… No one ever noticed the strange happenings the entire year.

The lights disappearing at the ball, the awful unpredictable weather and how extreme it was on certain days…

Everyone felt a twinge lighter in weight than usual, as light as air. Small feathers of birds started to float three or maybe even four inches above the ground, but it happened so slowly, starting with little things like the weather to what extent? But no one knows.

Yet…

Which brought them to a whole new realm of scary.

But she was not going to focus on that right now. It was holiday time. And there was always room for fun!

CHAPTER NINE

HAPPY HOLIDAYS HAZEL

This year, Mr. and Mrs. Halley had gone to visit Aunt Amelia and Uncle Jenner, and so, Hazel would spend the holidays at school, along with Hannah and Rebecca.

It was a wintery morning and the dormy was full of snores. Hazel was still in her nightdress as she stared out of the window. The weather was bitter cold, there were icicles and huge snowflakes fell gently to become a part of the white, fluffy bed of snow below.

'At least half the school isn't frozen like last year, thanks to some crazy comet,' Hazel thought happily.

Nothing to look forward to. Other than exams. But they were two months from now and there was really no need to worry.

There was a bright green fir tree fully decorated and the baubles gleamed brightly. That's when Hazel remembered that it was Christmas and she should do some shopping today so that she could keep some presents under the tree.

After dressing up, she went to the Great Hall with Hannah and Rebecca. It was decorated with the largest most beautifully decorated Christmas tree Hazel had ever seen.

It was so gorgeous with the tinsel, candy canes, lights, ornaments, fairy dolls, little Father Christmas', baubles, stars, ribbons, streamers and popcorn chains(she would have to remember to keep Hannah away from it, or else she would eat it all up).

There was fake snow on the floor and exploding crackers and gingerbread cookies were floating around the Great Hall.

Some of the choir students were singing carols, conducted by Professor Potts, who grinned heartily.

Hazel sat down and wished all her teachers a very merry Christmas, and gave a little smile in Snoddy's direction before running off to give

Christmas cards she made to Professor Potts and Miss Pennywood, her two favourite teachers.

Then, she sat down on the second form tables with Louella and Clarissa.

"I'm going to go Christmas shopping at eleven-thirty, so who want to come with me?" announced Rebecca.

"I can't as I simply couldn't affo…" Hannah stopped midway through her sentence and turned very pink.

"What I *meant* to say was that all my gifts are handmade," she corrected herself. "Therefore, I don't need to go."

"I'll come," said Hazel.

"Me too!" chimed in Louella.

So, the three of them left to go to Starmade, after seeking permission from the Headmistress, Miss Pennywood.

Hazel bought a holiday planner for Rebecca, so that she and Hannah could have a laugh watching Rebecca plan out every second of the day, along with a bookmark.

A box of chocolate gumballs for Hannah, along with brownie bites and chocolate fudge. Hannah loved chocolate.

An aftershave for Mr. Halley, a set of handkerchiefs for Mrs. Halley, teddy bears for the twins, a gift hamper from Wonkers for Holly, the largest, most boring book for Fay and a nice warm blanket for Annie.

Satisfied with her choices, she skipped to the Post Office and got it wrapped in icy blue wrapping paper with snowmen on them, and a shiny red bow on the top of each present. Then, it was sent off to be delivered to her family.

Returning to the school with Rebecca and Louella(who had lost her purse after buying a toy car for her brother Ben).

Hazel dashed towards the common room, where all her presents were kept. She peeked under the Christmas tree, which was near the fireplace, to search for her presents.

A fancy quill set from Rebecca, a sweet little Christmas card from Hannah, a warm jacket from Mr. Halley, fifty-pence from Fay, a card from the twins, a cool Jack-in-the-Box which sung carols from Holly and a beautiful red hand-knitted scarf from Mrs. Halley, along with some mince pies and tarts.

She wished that Fay wasn't her sister at times. She wished that Fay would have a sense of humour and fun. But Fay was just as boring as ever.

Rebecca seemed to be a miniature Fay. "I've got to go to the library!" she said, and dashed off while Hannah and Hazel burst into fits of laughter.

"Shall we go down and have a snowball fight?" giggled Hannah.

"Gee, yes!" replied Hazel and then they ran down, squealing.

They started building a snowman, rolling up the very-easy-to-roll snow and built a nice, fat body. While Hannah fetched a carrot for the nose and five sizes too small gloves and an overlong scarf, Hazel found some lead and draw his features along with a moustache and beard.

It did look comical. Hazel and Hannah finished making the weird snowman and decided it was time to build snow forts. Hannah build a massive snow fort while Hazel ran for refuge behind a rock.

There was colossal effort applied on both sides, but then, Hannah had an idea. She crept out of her fort and ran behind the large rock and pelted Hazel with snowballs!

Hazel immediately ran and captured Hannah's fort! But then again, Hannah got the upper hand by climbing on top of the rock and started throwing snowballs from there.

And she slipped, falling on the snow which was piled up feet high above the ground, laughing.

Hazel seized her chance and rolled on top of Hannah who wriggled like a worm. After an hour or so, both the girls collapsed on the ground and made their snow angels.

Rebecca, Charles and Henry joined in the fun, and they all had a wonderful time.

"Err… Hazel, did you get my Christmas present?" asked Charles, tentatively, when they headed back up to the school.

"You mean that little gift in blue paper and ribbon, that was totally smudged? No, as I wasn't sure if it was mine. And did you and Henry get my presents?" replied Hazel.

"Yes, that watch was really shiny and nice, I liked it. Henry loved his tie too. He needed a new one." Charles said.

She went to her dormy again and unwrapped Louella, Pamelle and Charles's gifts, which were many different sweet boxes.

"Ooh, thank you everyone!" gushed Hazel. "And Rebecca, my mum allowed me to stay at your place for the summer!"

"That's great! If only I could come… I stayed at school during these holidays for you, and my parents would be upset if they don't meet me." Hannah said.

Hazel and Rebecca understood. But they were a little disappointed that Hannah couldn't come. It was a blow!

CHAPTER TEN

WEATHER AT WAR

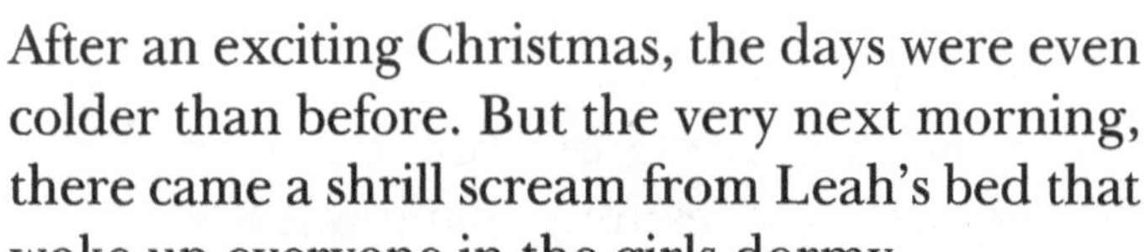

After an exciting Christmas, the days were even colder than before. But the very next morning, there came a shrill scream from Leah's bed that woke up everyone in the girls dormy.

"Yesterday, I swear it was at least -20 degrees! Today, it's hotter than the Sahara Dessert! What is going on?" said Leah.

"I got to know that because yesterday, water in the glass I keep next to my bed was nearly frozen and today it is so hot that it evaporated!" said Kaltheen.

"Yes," agreed Dorris, Amelia and Summer, the other girls in the dormy.

Kaltheen's golden hair were as golden as the sunlit corn and she had a wonky nose.

Amelia, who was the only African-American in school, was thin like a beanpole. She wore cat's-eye red spectacles and braces.

Summer was hot, and not because her name was Summer. She had sandy hair and soft brown eyes.

Dorris was tiny, with watery blue eyes and a tiny rosebud mouth with a heart-shaped face.

Leah had light brown eyes with flecks of gold and extremely pretty blonde hair. She was one of the most popular girls in their year, yet one of kindest girls Hazel ever knew.

She, however, was mystified. She knew there was something going on. But it was only four. Maybe she was dreaming that it was hot.

She pinched herself. It wasn't a dream. She feared it had something to do with the Comet of Ice.

'But it was a comet that spread ice and cold, not heat,' she argued with herself.

Her stomach jiggled like jelly. She went to the Great Hall for breakfast and put strawberry jam on her bread, but she could hardly take a bite.

"I know what you're thinking, Hazel, but you need your energy," said Rebecca, dumping all the porridge and baked beans on her plate.

"I'm not hungry," said Hazel, flatly refusing to eat.

"Just a little bit of buttered toast, or cornflakes," Rebecca pleaded.

"No!" Hazel snapped and left the Great Hall.

She lay down on her bed, tossing and turning.

Hannah and Rebecca came in. "Oh Hazel, it's not your fault that this is happening! It's… it's just a coincidence." Hannah said.

But that became harder to believe. The next day, there was a thunderstorm. Then, a rainy day and then a snowy day.

Hazel pressed her pointed nose against the frosty window, on which the snowflakes had formed delicate patterns. She knew it would thaw the next day and there might be a draught or a downpour; the weather had a mind of its own!

'If I hadn't stopped the comet, then it would be normal…' she thought. 'Normal! What if the Hallowe'en party was cancelled because of… me…? What if that lightning storm was more than just bad luck?' and the more she tried to swallow the truth of the matter, the guiltier she was.

Hazel didn't come in the Great Hall. She was so scared of the happenings around her.

She barely said a word. She couldn't even digest a second helping of Planet Pastry!

Millicent and her gang looked as if they won a lottery. She had no idea what upset Hazel, but it made her gleeful. These holidays certainly didn't turn out well for her, but she tried to act tough in front of Millicent, or she would crow over her like anything, and that was much worse.

Rebecca decided to take matters into her own hands. Hannah tried to be optimistic, but she knew Hazel would see through that at once and took a different approach.

"Look, even if you started this 'mess', you can stop it. Besides, what is wrong other than strange weather? How can you prove it really was your fault? Anyway, you didn't know what would happen. You did well and tried to stop the comet. You shouldn't accuse yourself without any evidence. Even if it was your fault, which I'm sure it wasn't, you didn't know this would happen."

Hazel gaped at the blunt honesty in her words. She didn't have a reply to one of them, let alone all the excellent points Rebecca stated. Honestly, it was worth reading a Guide to Everything in Space(it was a mundane thirteen-thousand-eight-hundred-ninety-seven-page long book) which only Rebecca and Fay managed to read without losing their sanity.

Perhaps it would do her good. Till then, she stood with her mouth open.

"You can swallow a fly!" Rebecca remarked.

A slow smile stretched across her lips.

"You smiled!" Rebecca exclaimed.

"Gosh, I did. Perhaps I might have come back to my senses."

"Good to hear, now come on."

A whole three days celebrating her own pity party! That certainly won't do, and Hazel was determined to cover up for that, winter holidays were much too precious to waste.

"HEY! TUFTY! Listen, I have an idea. I'm to the library to do a little research on the same, why don't you err… join me?" Rebecca said.

"Err… alright!" Hazel replied, brightly.

"I found nothing, yet," said Hazel. "But I'll keep on trying!"

Rebecca smiled patiently.

She smiled brightly and thought that it really was time for a trick on Millicent. If she wanted to stay at school in the holidays to bully Hazel, she'd have to face the consequences. She was so busy being upset, she didn't notice Millicent, the big bullying git.

"Listen, Hannah! I ordered some gun powder which I can mash up into a paste which blows up, once it is in someone's mouth. Becca gave me the formula to tweak that. So, your job is to sneak into the bathroom, nick Millicent's toothpaste, squeeze it all out, and fill it up with this gunpowder, which will explode in her mouth!"

"Yes, a delightful trick! Do you think that Rebecca's formula is correct?" chirped Hannah, examining Rebecca's most complicated diagram.

"Do you know Sniffles? Becca has never ever made a mistake. I'd be astounded if she had. Plus, I trust her," came Hazel's calm and confident reply.

"I thought that we could also put some itching powder in Grace's pants! And oldie but a goodie!" said Hannah.

"While Merlin's Mushroom's, you're jolly well right and we have a fake spider just ready for our dear, sweet, sensible Lottie. Imagine her face when she opens her pencil box, only to find a GINORMOUS spider staring at her!" chuckled Hazel, with her stomach aching with laughter.

"I'm happy you're back to normal Hazel! I thought only eggheads like Sniffles found solace in the library!" Hannah said. At these words, Hazel turned quite pink.

"Mind if I take the back seat? I still think reading a book would be better," stated Rebecca.

"Okay Sniffles!" said Hannah, rolling her eyes.

"Well, I was thinking of Sneezing Sunflowers for Ruby. A little bit of humiliation is just what she deserves and for Stella, I want to spoil those golden locks of hers that she's so vain of." Hazel giggled.

"Yes! We can put some Jump-Out-Jack-Powder and Starshine on a pair of scissors. So, we can wrap it up in a pretty little box with a ribbon on top and say in big bold letters, 'A gift for Stella from her secret admirer who loves her beautiful gold curls!' Haha!" laughed Hannah.

"And when she opens the box, the scissors will chase her and chop off her lovely hair! Amazing! Sensational!" cried Hazel, with a laughing fit to burst.

"Operation, started," said Hannah.

Hazel nicked Millicent's toothpaste and filled it with the Gunpowder paste, which was the same foul, charcoal black colour as her original toothpaste. She also put itching powder in Grace's pants.

Hannah scattered some Sneezing Sunflower Seeds on Ruby's seat in the Space Science classroom, knowing that Miss Pennywood's reaction to such nonsense would be the most hilarious and put a fake spider in Lottie's new yellow pencil box, which she left in her drawer. There were some broken quills and ink bottles in it.

Hazel went to the student's store cupboard in the Reflections classroom and created the formula to enchant the scissors. Then, she wrapped it neatly in a box with that stupid 'secret admirer' note, knowing that Stella's vanity would get the best of her.

So, In the morning, Millicent woke up.

"Hello me," she said, admiring herself, combing her hair.

Then, she picked up her toothpaste and smeared it on her brush.

Dab, dab! She wet the brush a little and put it in her mouth…

KABOOM!

The gunpowder exploded, and her mouth was on fire. Millicent panted, the searing pain in her mouth increased by the second.

"Why, dear Millicent, are you looking for an antidote? That mouth of yours looks like it's on fire. I've got the Deluxe Deflating Draught Dabbler. But you've got to say, 'Please give me the antidote Hazel,' in your sweetest most polite voice.

"I've got the camera rolling; you'll get the fame you want Millicent. Charity will love to get her hands on this video," said Hannah with an evil grin.

Millicent made a grab for the antidote, but Hazel was too quick for her. "You little wretch! It's all your fault! I'll pulverize you! I swear, you two-faced beast!"

"Film all of it, Hannah!" cried Hazel in victory.

Millicent had no choice but to do what Hazel wanted. Knowing that she was going to be a laughing stock if she said what Hazel wanted out loud, she mouthed the words.

"Sorry, couldn't her that." Hazel sang in an aggravating sing-song voice.

Millicent said it again in a hoarse whisper. Her tongue couldn't take the fire much longer.

"It seems as if my ear is clogged, speak up, *please*." Hazel said and both knew perfectly well that her ear was perfectly alright.

"WILL YOU PLEASE GIVE ME THE ANTIDOTE?" shrieked Millicent on the top of the lungs. She could worry about the video tape later; she need the antidote right now.

"Here you go!" giggled Hannah, tossing the tiny bottle to her and off both the giggling girls went to shoot Grace's disgrace.

Grace was having a fit. Her head was spinning, the nails digging harder in her flesh, her skin was going to peel off if this dangerous itching didn't stop!

She spun and spun, her body itching madly, and rushed to Matron as she heard the squeals of delight from Hazel and Hannah, knowing that Grace was making a mountain of a mole hill. The skin was slightly red, as the skin scorcher in the itching powder was added in limited quantities.

"Ooh, it's time for Space Science!" Rebecca giggled and went to the classroom.

Ruby was late as usual, and got detention right away. She strutted as she sat down and the action started.

"ACHOO! ACHOO! ACHOO!" Ruby couldn't stop sneezing.

The class giggled. "Pooh!" said Susan. "Do grab a hanky Ruby, you're sneezing all over me."

"Who was it? Disrupting the class like that?" Miss Pennywood thundered. Hazel and Hannah pointed at Ruby (as Rebecca preferred taking the back seat when it came to tricks).

"Detention Ruby! It was a disgrace and double detention for not confessing!"

Ruby scowled, turning beetroot red and buried her face in embarrassment.

"Ok class. Please open you pencil boxes and do exercise 10.2 questions 1,2,3,4,5 and 6 in your exemplar on page ninety-seven.

"AAH!" came a scream from Lottie.

"Ouch! My ears! Have got any sense Lottie? It this class a madhouse?" cried Miss Pennywood.

"B... but... but..." stammered Lottie.

"But what?" said the exasperated Miss Pennywood.

"There is a spider in my pencil box!"

"Pick it up and throw it away! It can't harm you!"

"But I don't like spiders!"

"Urgh! Belinda, do it for her!"

"No ma'am, I'm afraid of them myself."

"Hazel please do it for her. Please, I beg you! I want this class started!"

"Yes ma'am," said Hazel, meekly, knowing that the spider was a fake.

"And you, Lottie, can serve double detention for a month every day for two hours, or you can stay for two days in the Hall of Horrors," she said, now in such a bad mood, it looked as if she were about to explode.

Everyone knew about Miss Pennywood's raging hot fiery temper which was ever so rare.

Hazel longed to know what was inside the Hall of Horrors, a forbidden area, even for the teachers. It was believed that the hall was haunted. It was so dreadfully feared that no one had ever gone inside and Lottie didn't want to be the first one to and chose to do the detentions.

She heard it was scary. Hazel heard a rumour that last year, a third-year student went in the Hall of Horrors and was never the same again.

Only the Headmistress was allowed to punish the students by letting them go in the Hall of Horrors, otherwise Snoddy would have locked all three girls there for all eternity if he could.

Hazel and Hannah thought it would be fun to mock her at it.

She was forced to scrape off tubeworms from the girl's bathroom.

Hannah got the best of her by hiding behind the door and when Lottie sneaked in the bathroom so that no one would notice, Hannah burst into gales of laughter, along with the other girls who also hid behind the stall doors.

"I think this is a bit cruel," said Rebecca, doubtfully. "We should stop."

"No way!" laughed the other girls.

"Stop being such a goody two-shoes Rebecca!" said Charlotte.

"Yeah, you're a saint!" Summer agreed.

"Ooh, my ribs hurt! I'm simply dying to put that box on Stella's bed!" choked Hazel.

"I'll do it," said Hannah.

Soon, the box was placed on Stella's bed.

Stella squeaked when she read the overly buttered note. "Ooh, I wonder if it's Marool, or Roger or maybe... Kelvin! I just knew he admired this golden sheet of beauty, which is almost agonizing to take care of! But I did get a good price. Millicent and the rest of my friends do seem to be a little jealous of my hair and all. Just wait until I show them."

"Such a spoilt brat," said Hazel, disgusted.

"What a drama queen!" said Rebecca, astounded. "She's so full of herself, I'm surprised her head hasn't toppled over!"

"I don't know all of that stuff, but this is priceless!" whispered Hannah.

And so, Stella swooned and batted her lashes and slowly open the box.

She only had time to scream with horror and run for her life as the enchanted scissors leapt out of the box and chased her!

Stella ran and ran, sobbing all the same. She zig-zagged across Hazel and her friends, trying to dodge a particularly wild attack from it.

"Watch out Becca!" warned Hazel.

"Thanks," panted Rebecca.

They had a wild chase, and the scissors put up a very good fight. Since Hazel added an Attraction Amplifier as well, it was only attracted to Stella.

Stella panted. Her once long hair that reached till her waist were only till her shoulders. They weren't cut evenly either, and looked jagged.

Hazel quickly sprinkled some Repelling Pole Powder(Rebecca explained it would counter the magnetic properties of the Attraction Amplifier, etc.) which made it stop at once, while Stella ran to Matron.

"Irresponsible, personally, Snoddy should be sacked. Honestly, Reflections should be banned. Students mixing up all sorts of potions or whatever that is, students mixing unknown Reflections, twisting that into jokes, completely out of the question, in my opinion. Anyway..." Matron complained as she sprinkled essence of Spring flowers, Daffodil Petals and Sunflower Seeds on her hair, which made it grow back at once(she was determined to find a good hair remedy after what happened to Hazel last year).

"Oh my, those jokes are funny!"

"I agree, I loved Lottie's reaction to the spider."

"Nice joke Hazel!"

"Now, what is the time?"

"Uhhh... seven thirty..." Rebecca replied, checking her watch.

"Oh no! I need to go to the library! What about my dinner?"

"You go, I'll get some dinner," said Hannah.

"Thanks Snickers, bye!"

CHAPTER ELEVEN

A KEY WITH NO CHEST HAZEL AND MILLICENT PROV

Over the next few days, Hazel's hair were getting all bushy and puffy. She spent hours in the library, grabbing the books madly.

She skimmed through a particularly thick novel, flipping through its dusty pages. Nothing…

She gave the book to Rebecca, who immediately started to scribble furiously, clearly, she was making some scientific mumbo jumbo annotations. Nope, nothing would help. It was all a scrambled mess.

"Gravity… core… portal… hall… rings…" she kept muttering.

"Hazel, I don't know what is this yet, but the key to this mission has something to do with these words."

"Let me look at that!" Hazel jumped with excitement.

She preened in. "I think there is some sort of portal in the Great Hall that leads us somewhere."

"I brought dinner!" came Hannah's voice. "I know you dumped those sausages Tufty and I know you love chocolate chip cookies, chocolate cake, chocolate fudge, chocolate truffles, chocolate everything! Becca, you're a pig on sardines, banana muffins and strawberry swirl. I got all that!"

Hazel's mouth was as brown as mud, Rebecca's cheeks were as pink as pigs and Hannah crunched on her crackers.

"We found something very interesting." Rebecca said, showing Hannah her calculations.

"Maybe it's a secret passage. That's like a portal." Hannah suggested.

"Time!" Rebecca exclaimed. "The pieces of the puzzle are plopping into place!"

"Huh?" Hannah asked, confused.

"Well... I studied a bit, gravity doesn't pull things down, it pulls it towards itself. So there would be a core. Like an apple seed in the middle. Then there can be some portal to the core..."

"Oh, come on Hazel. Let's go now. Every time you have a doubt, you can't plop yourself on to a beanbag, just because you can't solve it. You may have noticed that that the word 'can't' has a can in it. Just use some of that gunpowder you used on Millicent to knock off the *t* in it," said Hannah.

"You're right," replied Hazel, and they hopped to the Great Hall to look for secret passages and portals.

They poked and prodded with great hope, but alas, there was no portal.

"Maybe we are searching in the wrong hall!" said Hannah. "Or you have to say some secret code. Tap at the walls! Pull the tiles to find a trapdoor! There's got to be something here!" Rebecca argued.

"There's nothing here," yawned Hannah.

"WE HAVE TO CONDUCT AN INVESTIGATION! FOCUS!" Rebecca shouted at Hannah.

"HEY! NOT MY FAULT THERE'S NO DUMB PASSAGEWEY!" yelled Hannah.

"Maybe you could…" said Hazel, meekly.

"BUTT OUT, TUFTY!" said Hannah and Rebecca, firmly.

"YOU DON'T KNOW WHAT WE MIGHT FIND *HERE*!"

"MAYBE ITS SO OTHER HALL!"

"JUST BECAUSE YOU HAVE WOOL AND DEAD FLIES FOR BRAINS, DOESN'T MEAN WE ALL HAVE!"

"AND NOT ALL OF US ARE BRAINIACS LIKE YOU!"

"SHUT UP!" roared Hazel, grabbing their sleeves.

"LET GO, TUFTY!"

"WE HAVE GOT BIGGER TROUBLE, SO FOR ONCE IN YOUR LIVES, HOLD YOUR TONGUES!" said Hazel, exasperated.

Hannah and Rebecca merely huffed.

"FINE!" she shouted. "I'LL DEAL MILLICENT ON MY OWN! HELLO? I'M SAYING THAT I'LL DEAL MILLICENT ON MY OWN!"

"ALRIGHT!" said Hannah and Rebecca.

Hazel stormed out of the Hall.

"Hi Hazel! How's everything going with your pathetic little friends?" sneered Lottie.

"It surprises me that you're the one to ask this, Lottie, looking at the company you keep."

"Puh-leeze! We're way better off than you!"

"Yeah," said Millicent, strutting up the Hall.

"Today was fun, wasn't it Millicent?" Hannah said, slyly.

"YOU MEAN BEAST!" screamed Millicent in fury. "I know you did that; I know you did. I'm going to Miss Pennywood! AND ALSO, BETTER WATCH YOUR STEP CAUSE I'M GOING TO GET BACK AT YOU ALL!"

"I doubt she'd believe you," said Hazel in a bored voice. "Our tricks are way beyond that."

Literally screaming with rage, Millicent exited the Great Hall.

"Good job," said Hannah, gleefully.

"Yeah, me and Hannah sorted it out...," said Rebecca. "We couldn't leave you to deal with Millicent and her cronies all alone. Maybe my calculations are incorrect."

"As if! You've got more brains than the entire school! Only Fay Halley could beat you to it." Hannah said. "Maybe the passageway is somewhere else."

"Yeah, let's get some sleep," yawned Hazel.

The next day was sunny.

"Is it really that sunny April month in January, or am I hot?" asked Hannah.

It was shocking. At first, nobody noticed anything until Leah had screamed a few days ago. Now, it was the daily gossip.

***

Millicent hated this lowly academy, right from day one. Her father refused to transfer her to a new day school, because Starway Academy was the only academy which taught about Space.

But apart from Halley and her friends, there were other people who found new and beastly ways to make her life miserable.

Charity of course, had gotten hold of that embarrassing prank! The horrible woman had plastered that article on every tree in Starmade!

Hazel was pleased, much to her fury. "Thanks Charity, we owe you one!" she'd sang.

Millicent could do nothing but keep a low profile.

Miserably, Millicent went out to Starmade, her nose stuck up in the air.

But that beasty woman, who Millicent had thought was a useful ally, had betrayed her. And now she was suffering this great humiliation. Charity was going to be sorry for what she did. Her day was ruined!

***

Hazel, Hannah and Rebecca however, had a blast! They went to the grounds, with the little butterflies and squirrels welcoming them.

The snow became crunchier and slushier. It was as if spring were about to come!

The trio had a snow picnic. Rebecca neatly laid out a very thick blanket over the snow and placed another one over it.

"I suppose the exams are starting soon," Rebecca said.

"Let's enjoy the last day of peace, while we can." Hannah muttered to Hazel.

The next week, everyone forgot about the crazy weather. They poured over their books.

All the students seemed to be in a frenzy in a library.

Rebecca had a freak out. She hadn't slept for five days.

"HOW ARE YOU SO RELAXED?!" she madly shrieked at Hannah.

"But what about the secret passageway?"

"NO TIME!"

"Ok, now, Becca, breathe, slowly…" Hannah said.

Rebecca panted and sniffed.

"You can test me," said Hannah.

"What is Dark Matter?"

"What's Dark Matter again?"

"You'd fail for sure!"

"Nah, I'd copy you."

Rebecca madly threw a book at Hannah, knocking her down.

"CALM DOWN!" screamed Hazel.

"Grow until you can, but don't grow until you drop. I think you've lost your touch, Sniffles." Hannah said.

Finally, Rebecca caught hold of herself, shaking and acting oddly.

On the day of the exam, Hazel as usual, passed all her subjects with distinction. Hannah lost her head on Space Science, but other than that, she did well, even in Reflections!

Rebecca as usual passed with flying colours, it was no surprise.

Finally, only Aliens exam was left. Hazel furiously scribbled on her parchment, and finished before Rebecca! But then, she always beat her in Aliens, as Rebecca loathed creatures, animals and outdoor activity.

To her surprise, she got an E in Aliens! "You didn't even take your exam, how can I even remark on it?" the Report Bee said.

Millicent smirked, holding a bottle of invisible ink!

Hazel raged with fury, and pounced at Millicent. She would have beaten her black and blue if Hannah hadn't held her back.

It was a good thing Hazel didn't strangle Millicent, because Professor Potts arrived.

"Ah, Hazel! I know you must have scored well in Aliens, didn't we? Anyway, I wanted you to know that there is another match in Surfwink you're bound to win! You're playing against Dr. Sprocket's School of Space! I know I shouldn't have told you, but if we do, we reach the semi-finals and maybe, win the cup for the first time in years! I'm so excited, for I was a Catcher too!"

Professor Potts looked so excited and wistful; Hazel felt that he'd be spitting rainbows next.

But she was disappointed with her score in Aliens and was determined to make up by winning the Surfwink finals.

She practiced hard, but couldn't concentrate, her mind still buzzing about the secret passageway.

"HAZEL, WHAT ARE YOU DOING!? A RING WAS RIGHT NEXT TO YOU!" Alicia screamed. Hazel turned red with embarrassment.

She wasn't looking for a ring, her mind felt so fuzzy and distracted.

That's when a sandy-haired opponent tossed one of those rings, which hit hard on her forehead.

She felt dizzy and the last thing she could remember was falling off her board.

Hazel had no idea where she was. All was blur. All she could make out was Alicia screaming.

"NOW, WE HAVE TO PLAY ANOTHER MATCH AND WE HAVE TO SCORE A HUNDRED MORE POINTS IF WE WANT TO REACH THE FINALS! NOW WE'LL BE PLAYING AGAINST THE KNIGHTLY EDUCATIONAL INSTITUTE OF NIGHT, WHICH IS PROBABY THE TOUGHEST TEAM YET!"

"STOP IT, ALICIA!" cried many voices. "Stop taking everything so seriously. Just chillax."

"Yeah Alicia," Hannah said. "When it comes to Surfwink, you're worse than Fay Halley, and that's saying something. Or Miss Bookbomb."

Rebecca blushed.

CHAPTER TWELVE

THE HALL OF HORRORS

A few minutes later, she woke up in the hospital wing.

"Dangerous sports, should be banned. What was Miss Pennywood thinking?" Matron was muttering.

"Ah, Hazel! You are going to stay here for the rest of the day."

"Yes, Matron."

She got up to get some cool night time breeze and was shocked to find out that the Sun was shining brightly in the sky!

"How is it... possible?" wondered Hazel.

She must be dreaming. Maybe, she just had to collect her thoughts. This was nothing.

"Hazel! Are you okay? We're sorry we didn't come here sooner; we only knew when miss pennywood told us you passed out and…" said Hannah and Rebecca in unison.

"It's alright, I'm fine."

"It's all my fault! I was so busy reading that I skipped the match which meant the world to you! I didn't even bother to find out how you felt about the same! I'm so sorry Tufty!"

"Chillax, ok? Take it easy, I said I'm fine!"

"Ok then, just checking." Hannah said.

They both had to leave for lessons, Matron had insisted.

The next day, Hazel was as fresh as a daisy. After a draining lecture about the Formation of Earth and exciting Star Gardening session, the girls started to explore Sirius, Hazel's favourite star. She loved watching it twinkle in the night.

Finally, they left for Space Science.

Miss Pennywood said, "Hello! Now Elwin, can you please pull up those blinds for some fresh sunlight? I really have no idea why Professor Snoddy teaches in the dark."

Elwin sprinted towards the window to pull back the curtain, and was shocked to find out that there was no day. It was night!

"We have got to solve this mystery," whispered Hazel.

"One strike for you Hazel. Any more of your chit chat will get you to the Hall of Horrors." Miss Pennywood said, angry and worried about the day and night cycle. If there is anything she couldn't stand, it was side talks.

Hall of Horrors. That triggered something in her memory.

"But then could it really be?" Hazel muttered, lost in her strange thoughts. The clue was hall. There are other halls as well. So what if the portal was in the *Hall of Horrors*?

Rebecca understood what she meant. Obviously. There was darkness in light but there is light in darkness as well.

Hazel knew she must annoy Miss Pennywood so much that she goes into the Hall of Horrors with Hannah and Rebecca and started whispering with them.

"Guys, what are you up to?" Louella asked.

"Girls, please stop..."

"Listen to Miss Pennywood..." pleaded Louella.

"Sorry Lou but you need to but out of this!"

"Yeah, you're ruining the plan."

"So, unless you want to go to the Hall of Horrors, you better stay put."

"Nuh, uh! I'm telling Miss Pennywood if you don't stop talking."

"NO!" screamed Hazel.

"YES!"

"No!"

"Yes!"

"Come on, Lou!"

"You come on!"

"GIRLS! INTO THE HALL OF HORRORS! HOW DARE YOU DISSRUPT THE CLASS? LAST YEAR, YOU WERE NEW AND YOUNG! YOU WERE ADAPTING TO A NEW ENVIRONMENT. YOU WERE CARELESS LAST YEAR! BUT THIS YEAR, YOU SHOULD GROW OUT OF IT! YOU REALLY ARE SUCH A TROUBLESOME LOT! NOTHING WORTH GIGGLING

ABOUT, YOU SHOULD BE ASHAMED OF YOURSELF!" she screeched, and sighed.

It was a tough day for Miss Pennywood and she was really not in her right mind. The water for her shower was too cold, her milk was too hot, she lost her favourite glittery brooch, somebody shredded her papers so she had to do all her work again.

Louella looked as if she had seen a ghost while the trio winked at each other.

The four, along with Miss Pennywood walked down towards the basement and she pressed a button which led down to a narrow staircase full of spiders and cobwebs. Then, they reached a tall, narrow hall and there was a heavy, locked door at the end of it.

"I shall come back in a few hours," she said curtly and left.

She shuddered slightly as she opened the door. Louella trembled and wept. The room was pitch black.

"Don't worry Lou, I have flashlights." Rebecca said.

This room was terrifying, the shadowy walls, the darkness, the strange noises, the eerie smell of burned charcoal, the sound of scraping fingernails and the fact that they were locked in the scariest room in the world.

"I'd thought it would be scarier," said Hannah.

"Me too," said Hazel.

"I guess it was just an exaggerated rumour that this room was haunted, now let's find it."

They dug for hours on the sandy floor. Louella was huddled in the corner, shivering. She wanted to go out and fast. She questioned what the girls were doing but they told her to ask later.

After sometime, Hannah felt her hand touch something cold and smooth.

It was an old oval mirror. So boring.

"You get what you get and don't be upset Hazel." Hannah said when she saw Hazel's discombobulated expression.

"Yeah, you can't turn coal into gold with a flick of a wand, it ain't work that way."

"What is this about?" asked Louella.

They had no choice but to explain. "Ooh, how exciting!" Louella said.

"Yes, Hazel thinks it's because of the Comet of Ice. I think the pieces of it might be the reason this is happening… just a wild assumption."

"Ok, now let's go through this portal."

"WAIT! I know what's happening. Last night while I was gazing through the Tremendous Telescope, I saw a something I couldn't put my finger on. It was visible only for a fraction of a second, but I thought, I'm not sure, but I think a saw a... a... ring, you know, like Saturn, those rings. And remember the clues the book gave us?"

"Yeah," said Hannah. "Gravity... core... portal... hall... rings..."

"Yes! So not all of the comet was destroyed! Some of the fragments escaped, so the *core* of the comet was still there and using *gravity*, it formed into a small planet with its *ring* system!"

"And this portal leads us to the Planet of Rings!" said Rebecca.

"But how can we destroy this planet about the size of the MOON?"

"Says the one who nearly destroyed Saturn," snorted Hannah.

"We don't have time for this!" Hazel yelled back.

But just then, the door opened.

"I hope you learned your lesson," said Miss Pennywood, as she unlocked the door.

"I guess we'll sneak in once we research about how to destroy the Planet of Rings." Hazel mumbled.

"We will start researching after a quiet weekend, I need a break." Rebecca muttered.

"Alright," said Hannah.

"I promise to keep it a secret, but in return, you're got to promise that you won't drag me into this crazy adventure."

"Fine, Lou," said Rebecca.

"Shhh... into your dormy, girls," said Miss Pennywood.

"Yes Miss Pennywood," chirped the girls. She was astonished to see them so happy.

After a day or two, things twisted for a turn. A huge blizzard, a blowout, the scorching Sun, a flood of rain and Miss Pennywood was in a frenzy.

"There is something wrong with this dratted weather. All Surfwink matches are cancelled until further notice. Don't go out unless you want to be a pig for slaughter, you're safe in the castle," she announced, gravely.

"THAT'S RUBBISH!" screamed Holly. "I WANT TO SEE MY SISTER CRUSH THOSE NIGHTY NIGHT GOOBERS!"

She was passionate about the sport and longed to see Hazel finally win. She had roamed around school when Hazel won her first match and boasted, came to congratulate Hazel and wolf down the cake.

"Guys, I don't think books are the answer for everything," said Rebecca.

"Says the girl who eats, drinks, breathes, sleeps and lives on books," snorted Hannah.

Hazel was tired of Hannah's 'says the girl who' jokes.

"Actually Hannah, I agree. Let's sneak into the Hall of Horrors, go to the portal and see where does it lead us to."

"But we can't destroy the planet, we need to know that first."

"Butt out, Snickers! I say we investigate; how do we know that this portal isn't folly?"

"But how, you know that only Miss Pennywood has the keys to open the door!" said Hannah.

"The stink bombs! They will be distracting enough to keep her out for a few minutes."

So, Hazel stink bombed the Headmistress's office.

When Miss Pennywood opened the door, she gasped.

"Ewww, what's that smell? I'll get some essence of lemon from Snoddy, that'll make my office smell more like lime!" she muttered as she left.

"HURRY!"

After rummaging her desk drawer, she found the forbidden drawer. She found the keys to the Hall of Horrors and put them in her pocket.

Inside were a few more things, odder than the next.

"Oh!" gaped Rebecca as she found a picture of mysterious purple fire. She tried to read its label, but it was smudged.

"HURRY!"

Rebecca ran out. "What is this?"

"Who cares about it, we have to go to a secret portal."

"Alright then, let's go to the Hall of Horrors first thing tomorrow."

They carried out the rest of the day as usual, giggling, chatting, trying not to mention the mystery they had to solve. They needed a break.

After that, they went to bed.

"Blaze... Blaze... Blaze..." came a soft voice in Hazel's dream. "What is this fire?" she reached out. That's when she saw a blurry image of purple fire.

"Blaze... Blaze... Blaze..."

"Oh shut up! I need to go and see the portal, find out how to destroy the Planet of Rings without causing imbalance in the solar system like last time and I don't want another mystery so LEAVE ME ALONE!"

The voice was so loud that she woke in a cold sweat. "What in the blazes is blaze? I better sleep." Hazel said.

"I had a strange dream last night," she announced.

"Me too!" said Hannah.

"And me!" said Rebecca.

"What did it say?"

"BLAZE!" cried all three at once. "NO WAY! WE ALL HAD THE SAME DREAM! I THOUGHT IT WAS ONLY ME!"

"That's because last time, you faced the comet alone, maybe this time, we three may have to face it together!"

"Now, let's have a decent breakfast. After that, you know where we'll go."

CHAPTER THIRTEEN

THE LILAC LABYRINTH

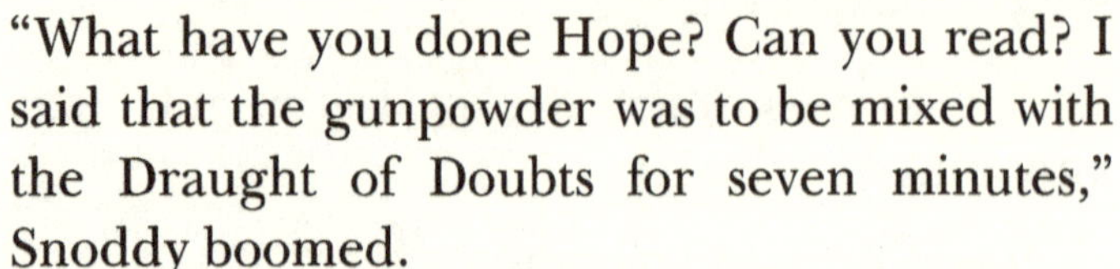

"What have you done Hope? Can you read? I said that the gunpowder was to be mixed with the Draught of Doubts for seven minutes," Snoddy boomed.

"Sorry Professor, it's a little hard to read from the back of the class. I thought that the seven was one." Hannah replied.

"Tut, tut, detention today, then."

Hannah knew she must go to the Hall of Horrors today.

"Err… I already have two detentions today." Hannah lied.

"We shall see, come to my office at four tomorrow evening."

"Yes Professor Snoopy, I mean Snoddy."

Snoddy raised his eyebrow and left, looking suspicious.

Another two lectures made by Miss Primsoll and Professor Fint.

"Let's go to the Hall of Horrors!" said Hazel, pressing the button. They ran down the staircase, hall and reached the door.

The girls rushed through the door.

"So, how do we get inside this mirror?"

"I think there is something written at the bottom.

"It says,

If you want to travel, touch me and just say where you want to go, but make it rhyme,

Or you will have to try another time,

If you want to come back,

All you have to do is repeat your rhyme and clap!"

"Strange riddle," said Rebecca.

"I think we have to say the name of the place where we have to go and if we want to return, we have to repeat our poem and clap," Snickers replied.

"Great, so where do we want to go?"

"The Planet of Rings?"

"No, there could be a thousand planets like that."

"What if we say this, we want to go to the place that will help us destroy the Planet of Rings, or basically, the place where the thing that can destroy the planet is hidden."

"Ok, so, portal, please transport us to the place where the weapon to destroy Planet of Rings is hidden."

"Why isn't it working?" asked Hannah.

"Look at the second line of the riddle, you dimwit." Rebecca snapped.

"It says that we have to make it rhyme."

"Ooh! I'll try!"

"No, Hannah."

"Gimme a chance!"

"Fine, go ahead but make it rhyme, I'm terrible at poetry."

"Take us to the place where the cure to the Planet of Rings is hidden, even if it is forbidden."

"That was an awful rhy... AAAH!"

A swirling mass of gold surrounded the three as they went swirling down the portal.

Hazel landed with a flump. Above her was a black hole that looked like a whirlpool.

"My head!"

"Ouch!"

"Where are we?"

"I don't know!"

"It's a maze of lilacs, a sort of labyrinth that leads to the weapon we use to destroy the planet of rings." Hazel said.

"Ok, so… how do we find our way through this maze? Where is it located?"

They looked around. The maze was enormous, impossible to navigate without a map. It had giant purplish-blue lilacs to make the walls. The stems were leafy green and tender, with dewdrops speckled on the giant leaves.

"This must be the Lilac Labyrinth! It is said that it's located miles deep beneath the school, lost forever, until now!" Rebecca squealed.

"Think of the rich history. The research. The clues about its founders. New advanced magical learning. New creatures, so much to study and learn. Think of all the re-reading and the re- re-reading!" Her eyes sparkled, looking longingly at the lilacs.

"Back to focus, we need to find a way to the centre. And when we are in danger, all we have to do is clap our hands and repeat the riddle we spoke to get here in the first place."

Hazel replied, knowing Rebecca would have already planned a long, droning lecture that would last for at least six hours.

Rebecca scratched her head, thinking of scientific theories. That is until she tripped over a Dazzler, which was a fiery yellow stone which connected to other Dazzlers, like fungi.

"Dazzlers are connected through their roots. So, there is a whole family of Dazzlers, which act like compasses, because they contain electyme, which is the substance that allows it to act like a compass. Their connection through roots is known as the Dazzling Network." Rebecca said.

"Exactly, so if they act like a compass, they should lead to the centre of the maze!"

"What a brainwave Tufty! Absolutely smashing, now come on, let's go!" Hannah said, as the trio ran, following the stones.

"We would have found these sooner if I just bothered to look around," laughed Rebecca.

A few were disconnected from the line of Dazzlers, but they were still able to follow it.

Rebecca struggled to pull out a Dazzler, with much twisting and turning, and needed the help of a pocket knife she had in her pocket. Underneath were thin red roots, which were warm and vibrating.

"That is because they connect to other Dazzlers, and there's a lot of vibration. After the Dazzler is pulled out, the roots turn grey, and become super powdery. In the end they crumble and just… fall off," Hannah said.

They followed the path for a while. The Dazzlers' trail came to an end. There were three doors and a sign with some writing on it

The first door was orange, the second green, and the third was purple.

Hazel removed the dusty sign and read aloud the shimmering gold letters.

Here you shall find three doors, but only one will let you pass. The second will trap you in a burning room, while in the third door, lies a bunch of Noxes. You can turn back right now, because if you dare to open any door, you shall be forced to enter it and it shall lock

itself so you can't escape. You can't use any form of magical teleportation magic to get you to safety, as the lilacs suck all of that magic to grow larger. Only if you pick the correct door will you return back, once you complete your quest. To help you pick the correct option, here is the clue.

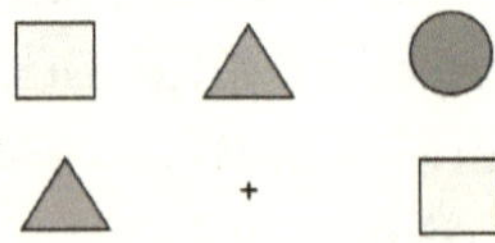

"So if we open any door, we'll have to enter it." Rebecca said.

"There is a yellow square, a blue triangle and a red circle. It says to add the square and triangle." Hannah said.

"I think it's the third door, why is it made of stone and the other two are made of wood?" Rebecca said.

"Use your common-sense, doofus. The fire would have easily burned down a wooden door. So they made a stone door," said Hannah.

"Move over, let me solve this." Hazel said. She examined all three doors, and exclaimed.

"There is a connection! The colours are all primary colours! It says triangle and square! Then we see there is a blue triangle and yellow square. So blue plus yellow gives me… GREEN! I think the green door is the path ahead, which is the second door." Hazel said.

"You're a genius!" Rebecca gaped.

CHAPTER FOURTEEN

BORN TO LEAD

Hazel opened the door and saw the path ahead. Now they must have completed the maze, since there were no lilacs or Dazzlers there.

A huge canyon was in their way. It was miles deep and all they could see was a tiny blue line crossing the canyon. It must be a river below.

"How is the sky present under the school?" Hazel asked.

"The labyrinth must have led us to this place, we must not be under the school anymore." Rebecca responded at once.

They saw three mammoth creatures flying above and they looked like dragons. "Those are Snapdragons! Those pesky plants!" Hannah said.

A Snapdragon whooshed pass them, but didn't notice the trio. It was about the size of a mansion with slender green skin, like the stem of a plant. Its tail was brown and was like a root. Its red eyes and tongue were vivid pink in colour, like petals. The beastly plant opened its ugly mouth which had a hundred teeth, identical to a Venus Fly Trap. A booming sound was there when it roared. A huge burst of red-hot fire issued from its mouth, with little sparks tumbling down like demons.

Two Snapdragons flew down and dipped their tails into the river and flew back up. "They use it to hydrate themselves like plants do, through their roots. Snapdragons are almost extinct, but they are aggressive and violent like dragons." Hannah said, amused.

"So we have to cross the canyon and be a Snapdragon's dinner if we're seen?" asked Rebecca.

"Yes," Hazel said.

"I'm scared," whimpered Rebecca.

"Think of a plan, Hazel," Hannah said.

"Hannah, you are the best at Space Gardening! You know everything about Snapdragons. This is your chance to show that you are the strong, brave, smart and confident girl that you are. You can do it!" Hazel said to Hannah.

"You and Becca are much smarter and better than I'll ever be at leadership. Just look at your quick thinking and Becca's wits!" Hannah replied.

"You are just as smart and talented as we are! Your unwavering loyalty is outstanding, and you are a genius when you think things through. I know you can do it, just trust yourself!" Rebecca encouraged.

"You believe in me?" Hannah asked.

"Of course we do!" Hazel said, incredulously.

"Ok, so Rebecca, use your pocket knife to cut some of those hanging vines. Hazel, tie it in the form of a lasso and hand it over to me." Hannah instructed. Hazel handed the lasso over to Hannah.

She waited until she saw a Snapdragon flying downwards. Hannah lassoed the rope and tied it to the beast's neck.

"Grab the rope!" Hannah said. "It's going to pull us down!"

The trio grabbed the rope and were pulled down until they landed on the Snapdragon!

It was violent and shook it's neck to let go. The three did not let go and Hannah controlled it with ease. Soon, they were flying across the canyon.

"I think all those were character tests… I had to stop thinking of theories and look around. Hazel had to apply some logic and observe while Hannah faced the greatest challenge of all. She had to step up and take the lead." Rebecca said.

"And we all passed with flying colours," Hannah said.

"Full speed ahead!"

Hannah enjoyed being the smart one for once. She was delighted and more cheerful. The journey was long, but soon they came to the other side, as it was a huge canyon.

They jumped off the Snapdragon, but Rebecca lost her grip and tumbled down the canyon!

Hanging on to a tree branch, she clung on for dear life. Hannah and Hazel managed to pull her up, but it wasn't an easy task. They walked away from the canyon, and reached a frozen pond. A fiery purple glow seemed to be coming from the centre of that large waterbody.

"It must be the weapon, heating up like fire…" Hannah said.

"FIRE!" cried Hazel. "Yes, yes, fire it is! A unique purple fire that appeared in our dreams! A fire powerful enough to burn a planet!"

"It must be Firefox; I now know that it is what blaze meant! I never thought of that, oh Hazel, it's beyond dangerous. I don't think we should use it..." Rebecca said, worriedly.

"THEN WHAT CAN WE DO?" Hazel yelled back.

"I don't know," Rebecca said sarcastically, rolling her eyes.

"Maybe learn from your lesson to THINK THINGS THROUGH?"

"Yeah right, that's in the past. Snickers, how do we dig this pond up?" Hazel asked.

"Jumping up and down the ice?" came Hannah's reply.

Rebecca refused point blank to help them.

"FINE! Just don't bother us then!"

"I don't know why I came to this freezing pond with Christmas trees all around and snow for you both! I nearly died minutes ago. I'm going back to Starway Academy..." Rebecca huffed and walked away, tossing her curly red hair.

"DON'T KNOW WHY YOU EVEN BOTHERED TO COME, ABANDONING YOUR SO-CALLED FRIENDS, RIGHT WHEN WE ARE ABOUT TO SAVE THE WORLD! ARE YOU REALLY THAT SELFISH?"

"Selfish?" Rebecca shrilly cackled. "I'm the one trying to save you from destroying everything including yourself! Look who's talking, no point in arguing for these petty things. I've got research to do."

And then she appeared to vanish.

"Come on Hannah, we've got more important things to do!"

"But I j... just c...can't stand us f... f... fighting..." Hannah said, tears pouring down her cheeks.

"Quit being a cry-baby for someone who abandoned her friends for selfish motives!"

"But what if she was right? What if the fire does prove to be dangerous? She was trying to look after you!"

"Yeah right, by abandoning us. Didn't I tell you a million times that I'm willing to take the risk to save the world, not for personal gain?"

Hannah had no reply. She helped her friend silently. The ice wasn't breaking. This was eating up their time.

Miss Pennywood would have immediately called her parents like last time. And this time she wouldn't be able to get away with the lie by faking that the call was for some other girl called Hazel.

That's when she saw Rebecca's shiny pocket knife glinting on the freshly fallen snow. Hazel glided towards the centre. She didn't slip, being an expert at it. Using the razor-sharp blade, she managed to make a hole to fit in one person.

"Now Hannah, I'm going in. If something goes wrong, don't jump in and risk your life. This is my mission. Don't go back to the academy, just grab a branch and lower it down so that I can get back up…"

"How long can you hold your breath?"

"For three minutes, I think."

"Good luck Hazel!"

And Hazel quickly dived in. The water was chilling, it nearly froze her to death. The pond was murky and dark, but she knew how to open her eyes in water. The cold sensation spread through her body, but she continued to swim deep down, following the path of the light emitted by the fire.

She struggled, her arms were nearly paralysed with cold and numbness was penetrating her like a seed soaking up water.

The light was warm, just like hope in darkness, She was getting closer and closer to this strange purple light…

It was Firefox, like Rebecca said, bottled up in the middle. Hazel reached out her hand to grab the fire, and tried to swim back up, but couldn't.

Hazel gurgled, "Hannah!" and started to sink like an anchor.

Hannah stood there in anticipation, and tore off a long, thin branch from a tree.

She put the branch in the water, waiting for Hazel to grab it.

Hazel clung to the branch with all her might and remaining strength. Hannah pulled her friend up with difficulty.

Hazel gave Hannah's hand a squeeze, and lay down. Hannah grabbed the bottle and put it near Hazel's cold white face.

Hazel smiled brightly. "You did it!" she cried with happiness, hugging Hannah as tightly as she could.

Their hearts fluttering with joy and happiness, they looked at each other intensely. The blue eyes found the hazel eyes, both smiling brightly.

"Let's not be that dramatic next time..." Hannah joked. Hazel laughed.

"Let's head back to Starway Academy. We need to use the portal again to go to the Planet of Rings." Hazel said.

Hannah recited the rhyme again and clapped. There was the swooping sensation as the gold light like that of the Sun, transported them back into their bellowed Starway Academy.

They were back in the Hall of Horrors...

CHAPTER FIFTEEN

THE PLANET OF RINGS

Their eyes adjusted to the dingy surroundings. The mirror was glinting at odd moments.

There was a dark shadow. It was towering and intimidating. It almost looked as if it were crying.

"Oh Hazel, Hannah, I'm so sorry that I left... I really wanted to come back the moment I left, and oh I just can't forgive myself... You were right..."

Hazel grinned. "What made you see sense so soon?"

"Right..." Rebecca said, her cheeks a deep crimson in colour. "Tom came and told me that there was an earthquake! I knew you'd come back soon... I was waiting... We're evacuating! The earthquake caused by the Planet of Rings is tearing the ground apart. I should have listened... At times, there is something worth the risk... But actually, I was jealous. I'm the one who come up with brainy and fabulous ideas all the time. I wanted to act like a wise owl and I proved to be stupid! If I had put my pride aside and listened..."

"No time for that mushy stuff!" Hannah complained. Rebecca nodded, meekly.

"Now let's evacuate! Hurry, hurry!" Hazel said, seeing the walls crumble.

"What about the mirror?" Rebecca said. "We'll have to carry it! I mean, it's not that large..."

The trio lifted the mirror and ran for their lives, watching in despair as Starway Academy, the school they loved, was crumbling apart.

They ran but a pillar crumbled down, causing the boys dormy to crack. So they took the long cut, down the other flight of stairs at the other end of the castle... Soon, they were encountered with a bigger problem. The stairs were crumbling as they climbed down!

"Surfs up!" yelled Hazel. She used the mirror as a surfboard and surfed down! Hannah and Rebecca ran.

"Hazel! This mirror won't break easily, as it's made of Cornide Sulphate, but please don't be so reckless!" called out Rebecca.

"Will do!" cried Hazel. Another wall and pillar broke. A huge 'wave' was coming, in Hazel's point of view.

"You are cool beans!" Rebecca said, giving a thumbs up.

Hazel began to slow down and landed outside with a big crash!

"What in the name of..." Miss Pennywood gasped.

"I can explain Miss..." Hazel panted.

"You used the forbidden portal... Yes Halley, I know all about it, I'm not letting you out of my sight, running after some wild comet again..." Miss Pennywood said with a twinkle in her eye as she spotted the mirror.

Hazel awkwardly stared at everyone gawking at her. "We are going to save the school... I request you to not panic..." she said.

"Miss, if I may use it?"

"The only piece of advice I can give right now; do what you have to do, and do what is to be done, Halley."

"Yes Miss," Hazel said.

"The planet that is destroying Earth is where I have to go,

Get me there fast; no time to be slow!"

The swirling light surrounded her and everyone stared, astounded, astonished and confused.

Hazel opened her eyes. Space was familiar-looking for her, and she stared at her toes turning into ice. And what mystified her was the fact she could breathe in Space without the protection of a Heartstone or a powerfully magical trinket.

She was standing on nothing, but she could feel a hard bumpy surface! Somehow, the Heartstone's vibrations, with its magical properties, made the Planet of Rings invisible! No wonder the world didn't know of its existence!

The rings were almost impossible to see, all Hazel could spot was ice spinning around, attracting more and more of the Earth, Rebecca was right about the rings' ability to attract matter(though she didn't pay much attention to it).

"HAZEL, HELP ME!" someone screamed. Strangely enough, her voice seemed to be coming from below the ground, but Hazel was too busy trying to figure out who she was and how the girl knew her name.

"Who are you?" she bellowed back.

"I DON'T REMEMBER, I'M TRAPPED IN HERE SOMEWHERE!" the voice replied.

Hazel thought the speaker was friendly, and had a playful note to her voice, but her tone was pure terror.

She couldn't burn down the planet with someone stuck there, could she?

Hazel decided to find the source of this mysterious voice. She walked for miles, though it was way too cold for sweat to trickle down her nose.

She came upon a rock with a golden key embedded in it. Hazel turned and twisted it in a zillion directions, but it wouldn't budge. She decided to check for a clue that might help.

And there it was, engraved on the bottom of the stone.

If you want to get something precious, you got to give up something equally precious.

With that unhelpful clue, she said, "What do I have to give up? I have nothing but myself."

Ignoring the clue, she continued trying to twist and pull the key, trying to wrench it out of the stone till her hand began to bleed, red drops dripping down the stone. To Hazel's astonishment, the stone became less heavy.

Immediately understanding the riddle, she smeared it across the stone, which vaporised right in front of her eyes, leaving behind the key.

Hazel gripped it tight; the spiky corners didn't hurt her anymore. She slipped it into her pocket, wondering what she should do next.

Just then, she felt vibrations everywhere, spinning, and cracking to form a cramped cubby of space. Hazel knew she should burn down the planet and go back when she had the chance, but there was something more sinister going on in there…

She went inside the cramped cubby and everything was just… wrong, somehow. Like how reflective the ice was, like mirrors. And shadows seemed to multiply, darkening the cubby hole.

Hazel traced her palm across the ice, staring at her own reflection, but it wasn't a reflection anymore, because it wasn't her face staring back at her, it was Hannah's.

"Hannah, what are you doing here? How did you get here in the first place?"

"Who's it?" Hannah asked.

"You can't remember?" Hazel exclaimed.

"Nope, it's kind of like a fog in my head. I can't remember a few things and my memory's fading." Hannah replied.

"Can you get out of here using the poem you invented and clapping your hands?" suggested Hazel.

"Nah, forgot what rhyme I cooked up." Hannah shut down that ray of hope.

"How can you breathe?" Hazel said.

"Cause I had the brains to think of bringing an oxygen mask." replied Hannah.

"Do you remember how you got in here?" Hazel pleaded.

"What's my name again?" she asked.

"Hannah!" Hazel said, angrily.

"Oh, right. Hannah-Banana or whatever my name is, tried to follow you, but some frowny girl called Molly, no... Minnie..."

"Millicent!"

"Oh right, that girl interrupted me and I said even prison was better than staying with her, made some sort of stupid poem out of it, and I got transported here, in this prison!" Hannah explained.

"How do I get you out of here?" Hazel asked her.

"I don't know, I don't know!" Hannah said.

"Come on Hannah if anyone can figure out how, it's you. I know you can do it!" Hazel said. "I'll help in any way I can, cause this is a two-person job. Have confidence like you did with the Snapdragon!"

Hazel could see Hannah racking her brains, trying to think of something, anything until...

"That key in your pocket, Hazel, I can see it from here. Use it to let me out!"

"How, there's no lock!" Hazel snapped.

Hannah scratched her head, her sharp eyes analysing the place for a few agonising moments until... Hannah blurted out, "I don't get this place. It's way too dark and the shadows keep multiplying by tenfold here unless..."

"What?" Hazel demanded.

"This place hides more than what you see with shadows," Hannah told her. "If you grab a reflecting object of some sorts, the lock will be revealed. Of course, that's the answer; light!"

Hazel rushed out of the cramped cubby and found a crystal. She held it up to the sunlight, which caused all the shadows to skitter away, revealing a lock.

She fumbled with the key as she inserted in the lock, only to find Hannah standing there, rubbing her head.

"I can remember who I am! I'm Hannah Hope! Thank you Hazel, I really don't know what I'd have done if you hadn't rescued me." Hannah said, as her memories flooded back.

"Nonsense, it was all your idea, I would have never thought of light and shadows as the answer." Hazel admitted, honestly, and laughed.

"Ready to burn down this planet?" Hannah asked an overly-exhausted Hazel, though she tried to hide her tired expression.

"Yep," Hazel replied. "You go, I'll be back in a minute."

Hannah nodded, repeated the rhyme and clapped her hands. WHOOSH! With a swirl of dust, she was gone.

Hazel opened the bottle and stared as the bright purple flames engulfed the planet.

She thought she saw dragons, snakes, lions, phoenixes, but the next moment was blur as the smoke made her head spin.

The world was getting dizzy and it was a matter of a few moments that the flames would reach her; but for a fraction of a second, she thought she saw a shadowy figure rise.

It wasn't truly flesh either, more like wisps of smoke forming the silhouette of man.

Hazel fainted. She was feeling dizzy and fatally ill. Tired and fatigued, she slumped down on the ground, ready to accept her fate.

This world was like a game for her; she made everything so fun, she was the one who brought hope when the world had none.

There was a faint moment where she thought she heard panting, a rock crash and a mirror smash.

She was not able to think. She was passing out. She knew she had no hope.

CHAPTER SIXTEEN

A TERRIFYING, YET TERRIFIC TERM

After a few hours, or possibly days, her hearing came back to focus. It was as if her brain nerves were connecting again!

Hazel thought she heard a sound of heartbeat. Quite familiar, but her body and mind were too weak to get up and see what was going on.

"Thank god she's okay!"

"Very lucky you could save her Matron!"

"I wouldn't if Miss Rose hadn't gone to save her!"

"But the mirror smashed when the door fell down, I thought I heard it break after I saved Hazel..."

"I think her life is more important than a mirror!"

"W... wh... at... g.. goin... g... o... n?" she croaked; her voice not even audible.

"You're okay! You were in a comma for five days... Your parents were informed this time, they're coming to visit." Rebecca said.

"Wh... ere a... re we?" Hazel asked.

"Charmwood Academy, we're sleeping in their place, and once the school burned down, we came here. You were transferred to their hospital wing." Rebecca said.

That is when Mr. Halley burst open the door and hugged Hazel. "Hazel, are you okay?"

Mrs. Halley added, "Your dad was worried sick! And I was too! What happened? Miss Pennywood told us some nonsense about a fire and the school crashing down! We came as soon as we heard you were in a comma!"

"I think it's best we leave them for the present moment," Miss Pennywood said, sweeping pass the doors with Matron.

"I just... um... fell down my board during a Surfwink match! The fall was brutal!" she lied, panicking, knowing that she'd be grounded for eternity if the truth was leaked out.

"Hazel Halley, I demand you tell me the truth! I am very well updated with your Surfwink routine." Mrs. Halley thundered.

"Be easy on her, what happened Hazel?" persisted Mr. Halley.

"Well..." said Hazel, seeing that she couldn't hide the truth. "It really wasn't Surfwink you see..."

"Mr. Halley, please don't be hard on her!" Hannah said.

"We can explain!" Rebecca explained.

She recited the fantastic adventure that she, Hazel and Hannah had. Rebecca told the tale in loving detail, especially the Hallowe'en ball and the Dazzling Network.

"Once you went through the portal, I knew Hazel wouldn't come back alone," Rebecca said.

"She was brilliant!" Hannah said, while Rebecca blushed scarlet. "She went after you and rescued you!"

"I saw it through the Tremendous Telescope. I saw you, and the flames, and I knew I should have never left you alone." Hannah said.

"Yep!" Hazel said. "Hannah, please continue..."

"Once Rebecca came back in time, that planet wasn't invisible! It was black and burned to a crisp! After a while, it crumbled into dust, so Earth got its mini ring system like Saturn."

"Don't be silly Snickers, the dust and debris flew away into Space, in the asteroid belt, near Mars, the Sun, Venus or maybe it flew off into the Kuiper Belt."

"Q-u-ee-per Belt?" asked Hannah.

"No! It's pronounced as K-i-per." Rebecca said in a matter-of-fact tone.

For some stupid reason the trio laughed at this. "It would be easier to continue the story…" Mrs. Halley said, angry and red-faced.

"Louella came to visit," Rebecca said. "All she did was knock over a cup of medicine Matron made for your wounds."

"Though, she gave you a get-well-soon card."

"Why do adventures end in hospital wings?" giggled Hazel.

"Is that really necessary?" fussed Mrs. Halley. "Now that was irresponsible, you should have reported this to a grown up!"

"Listen dear, I think you're being too hard on Hazel. I think saving the school was worth the risk, what matters now is that she's okay."

"George, you know very well it isn't something we should encourage!"

"Yes, but don't be so harsh with her."

"Hazel?" Mr. Halley said.

"Yes, dad?" she replied, staring into his hazel eyes and handsome features with worry lines.

"Promise me you'll try avoiding trouble and adventures in the coming years, we just want you to be safe."

"Usually, trouble finds me." Hazel smirked.

"Hazel…" Mrs. Halley said.

"That was very cheeky," Mr. Halley said, but winked slyly. He knew better than to argue with Mrs. Halley when she was in her rages.

"Sorry dad!" Hazel replied, winking back.

"I think I'll ask Fay to take better care of you… Or no, she's studying hard." Mrs. Halley muttered.

"Hazel, please stay close to Holly and write to me once a week or I'll think something has gone wrong!" she said, after a pause.

"Now we better get back home. Fay is coming with us as fifth year students' holidays start earlier than you do. Now we are proud of her exam results, but it would be nice to have a prefect in the family... The twins starting school next year... Anyway, enjoy Hazel!" Mr. Halley said.

Mrs. Halley squeezed the pulp out of Hazel with a strangling hug and left along with her husband.

"I really love you Hazel, and just want you to be safe." Mrs. Halley said, quietly. "I never mean to be hard on you, so just... tell me the truth, okay?"

Hazel hugged her and said, "Yes, mum."

They both were relieved and Mr. Halley was thankful there would be no more adventures for at least three months.

Hannah and Rebecca sniggered. "Well, that was some super smashing visit," Snickers said.

"I'll say!" Rebecca giggled.

Matron and Miss Pennywood came back. "Miss Rose, we have a letter for you."

"What does it say?"

She read the letter. "How lovely!" Rebecca said, slightly touched.

There was also a round parcel wrapped in brown paper and string.

Rebecca's face fell for a fraction of a second. "Oh! They sent a box of round chocolates; I can't say I'm fond of them."

"I'll finish them off..." Hannah said, popping two or three in her mouth.

"You're a pig, Hannah," Rebecca remarked.

"I'm just glad we three are going to be together again. But I really am distraught by the whole school getting destroyed." Hazel added.

She imagined the building, crumbled and broken. Everyone shed a few tears. It was their home and yet, they couldn't say a word.

Just then, Matron swooped in to check Hazel's blood pressure and saw their downcast looks.

"Starway Academy was really special," she said. "I know you're upset, but please cheer up, or Hazel won't easily recover."

"But it'll be rebuilt in the holidays. I heard Miss Pennywood say so." Matron said.

"Ooh, maybe we'll explore the school like we did in the old days; that would be fun!"

"I suppose our possessions would be lost..." Rebecca said. "But I suppose I really don't mind as long as we all are safe."

"Wait!" said Hannah. "If our possessions are lost, does it mean our pets are…"

"Oh no!" wailed Rebecca. She squeezed out a few tears and did her best to stop. Hannah was weepy, but she didn't want to show it.

"Oh well, he was a stupid old thing."

Hazel was heart-broken about Polly, but crying over spilled milk would do her no good.

"Ah, I would have to get a new trunk and I'll get a Winksey; yeah, I'd like that." Hazel could think of nothing else to say. But Polly was always going to be her favourite pet.

"I'll burst to tears if I see my trunk and Polly's birdseed hidden inside."

Rebecca was silent. Everyone was. A horrified expression adorned Hannah's face.

"How can I get a new trunk and an extra uniform? My parents won't be able to…" she asked.

"I can give you Fay's old trunk and hand-me-downs. The trunk will be old, a bit battered, and the uniform would be a bit large, but it would have to do." Hazel said.

"Thanks Hazel!" Hannah cheered up. That is when they heard a purr.

"TIBBLES?!" squealed Rebecca in delight. "You were in my sling bag?"

The kitten jumped in her hands and Rebecca cuddled her.

"Well, I guess we're reaching the end of the term…"

"I don't know why, but I feel blue and gloomy about it. I just hate the rush!"

"I suppose we'll enjoy easter next year. We'll be in the third form!"

"How grand!"

"Don't look like a dying duck, Becca, we'll be in the highest of spirits during the holidays. But I'd love to spend the first and last week with my family. I'm so cheerful the twins would come next year!"

Lessons continued for the next three or four weeks. Hazel stole an entire crate of ice-creams from the Charmwood Academy kitchens and shared it with her form.

Parents sent suitcases full of clothes, toothbrushes etc.

They all relaxed the next week; Charmwood students welcoming them and making sure they found their way around.

They stayed in the Trembling Tower, which was full of beds. The remaining students slept in the common rooms they had. All of them were pleasant, painted milky green.

The last day in the Trembling Tower was pandemonium.

"Hazel Halley, how dare you run off with my suitcase!"

"Why are you putting a picture of your parents in my bag?"

"That's my shirt!"

"Where is my grey sock?"

"Emily, please stop littering your stuff everywhere like plague!"

"Write to me, ok?"

And the fond farewells took place.

"Bye!"

"See you soon!"

"Bye!"

"You too!"

"Reply to my letters, will you?"

"Of course!"

"Enjoy!"

"Bye!"

"Same to you!"

And so on.

Hazel's face reddened with anger when she saw Charity. "Hi Hazel! Would you like to tell the world about your fantabulous adventure?" she said in a maddening sing-song tune, thrusting a mike under her nose.

"And would you like to get kicked out of here? Better leave me alone. I'll tell Miss Pennywood if I see you asking for an interview again!" she threated.

That gave Hazel a wicked idea. She secretly turned on the 'on' button on the microphone.

"But first tell me, Charity, why do you want to destroy people's reputation by twisting their images?"

"Gossip! Gossip, you little wretch! I want the juicy stuff! People aren't interested in those boring old facts! So what if I use deceit to twist them up a little? Add some spice to the gossip. No one wants to listen to some boring old teacher speak. They want to know the scandals; the scandals that will make me famous when I report them!"

"Fine! But you can't make up scandals on your own, Charity. More than gossip, people want the truth. And speaking of truth, whatever you're saying is being broadcasted for the entire world to hear!"

"How?" Charity asked.

And then she saw what Hazel had done. Her face reddened. Charity ran for it, muttering furiously. "I'll never forget this!"

But she couldn't care any less. Hazel waited for the bus to arrive; her parents couldn't pick her up as their car broke down. The grounds were larger than life, but not nearly as large as Starway Academy's!

They arrived at Charmwood Station(landing port) and waited.

The bus arrived at Charmwood Station and they boarded from there.

The trio chose a compartment near to Louella's. Their luggage was kept on the bed bellow Hannah's.

They said 'cheers' and licked their ice-cream. Tom, Charles and Henry entered. Rebecca was so surprised that she dropped her ice-cream and blushed furiously as she scooped it up.

"Sorry!" Charles grinned. "Tom wanted to return the book he borrowed from you Rebecca."

Tom smiled and nodded. He handed the book and went off with his friends. "Happy holidays!"

"Rebecca, you blushed so much that you're pinker than your strawberry ice-cream!" Hannah grinned.

"Oh blushy dear, I wouldn't be surprised if your cheeks turned into tomatoes. I can fry an egg!"

"They came and went like the wind! How can you blame me for dropping an ice-cream?" she fussed. Rebecca was really prim and proper when it came to dropping stuff, and was embarrassed that she spilled something for the first time in her life. That was usually Hannah's job.

Just then, the door opened again. Millicent gate-crashed. "Of all the poisonous toads!" Rebecca grunted.

Her usual sneer was there as she made fun of the trio.

Hazel's devious crafty mind worked as she thought of a madcap scheme.

She turned off the lights. Millicent said crossly, “Urgh, this place stinks too much. I’m outta here!” She didn’t want anyone to think she was scared.

Hazel grabbed the flaming candle and put it near Millicent’s bottom.

She sniffed. “AAAH!” she squealed in fright.

“I actually thought of my dad’s pants catching fire.”

“Well, let’s extinguish it before dear poky Pennywood comes.”

Hazel turned on the light and grabbed some water.

Millicent was baffled and frightened beyond words.

“I’ll get back at you for this!” she muttered and went to change her clothes.

The trio burst into laughter. Snickers composed a silly song which she rapped, making it more ridiculous than it really was.

“A really witty poem!” Rebecca clapped. “You really are a clever clogs, and a genius!”

“That poem suits dear Millicent to a tea!” roared Hazel.

After squealing for what seemed to be hours, they finally stopped.

"I nicked some stuff from the school kitchens. Here's a loaf of bread, some onions, cucumbers, tomatoes, lettuce, cream cheese, sizzling bacon which is not sizzling, cold ham, some chicken, pickles, pickled limes, sweets, chocolate cake, sweets, toffees, spotted dick, pink pork, gravy, applesauce, scrambled eggs and Planet Pastries!"

"Wow… who's going to eat that?"

"We'll save some for breakfast!"

The girls devoured half a loaf of bread, cutting the edges and making sandwiches, some bacon, ham and chicken. They ate a pickle each, pigged on the gravy, applesauce and sweets. They finished it off with lemonade and Planet Pastry.

Hazel ate a Uranus pastry which tasted like blueberry ice-cream. Rebecca daintily ate her Earth pastry which had a different flavour in every bite, while Hannah greedily gobbled a gigantic Neptune pastry.

They managed to resist the other leftovers and neatly packed them in a white cloth.

"What a smashing meal!" Hannah contentedly said.

Holly came in to share some extra food.

"Hello Hazel! I must say I'm proud that you had a reckless adventure indeed. I heard that mummy fussed over you and was furious and poor old dad managed to calm her down! Here's some extra food leftovers you'd like to eat. Now, I really must hear that fantastic joke Penelope is about to tell!"

She looked as if she wanted to bust, but kept a firm hand on her mouth. There was a mischievous twinkle in her eye and she did her best to hide it.

Hazel was not deceived. There was something fishy about her sweetness. Rebecca took an enormous bite of the banana muffin Holly sent, and she choked.

"This is a fake, I think so. It's impossible to chew!" she groaned. Indeed, that muffin was a fake. Hannah said that she thought she heard Holly's distant laugh and Hazel shrugged it off. Obviously Holly was laughing her head off!

Never mind, she'd get back at Holly in the holidays. Holidays, holidays, holidays was the only thing she heard! The students were in their highest spirits and danced with joy in their compartments.

Millicent was laughing, yes, laughing at a joke Marool recited, while Lottie chatted with Kelvin.

Stella, Ruby and Grace chose another compartment. Grace and Ruby gossiped, while Stella narrated mundane tales of her visit to Switzerland and Roger listened with much interest.

Louella was having epic pillow fights with her bestie Clarissa, her good friend Leah and her best friend, Marybelle. She had been awfully shy and timid, but she slowly crept out of her shell.

Other girls like Katie, Kaltheen, Adelle and Summer were singing songs and enjoying their last day together.

Soon, they reached the station. Hazel greeted the twins with a squeal of delight and a nice warm bear hug, as Anna put it.

Holly and Hazel made up and were as close as they were for they now went in their own separate ways.

Fay unexpectedly said that she would like to enjoy with her sisters because she scored full marks in SSAT and was promoted to seventh grade instead of mugging up with the old fifth formers.

They played Uno; an all-time favourite. Fay came last in the demo round, but got hang of the game very easily. Soon, she came in third place and young Ava was first!

Hazel was second, Anna fourth and Holly was last, as she was off her game that day, having swotted so hard for the exams. If she didn't, she would have been expelled, as she had failed in her first year exams as well. She did her best and merely passed, but she did get a score above eighty-two!

Knowing Holly's abysmal spelling mistakes, this was an achievement for her. It also qualified Holly to continue her education. Hazel felt sorry for Holly, a sentiment she never-ever felt for her before.

The twins were absolutely delighted for they were quite miserable without Hazel and Holly. When they demanded for their school stuff and a pet, Mr. Halley decided to go to Starway Street to get their school stuff at the end of the holidays.

Ah, well! She was going to Starway Academy in three months and staying at Hannah's home next week!

Goodbye Hazel! We're waiting to see what ingenious tricks you play next year. Happy holidays, you deserve them!

A NOTE TO MY READERS

Whoo! We made it through another Hazel Halley adventure!

I love writing the series, it's such an enlightening experience to expose oneself to the world of literature and Science combined.

The reason I started out writing this series is because I love writing, and I originally wanted to become a Space Scientist, so I thought, why not combine the two?

I also love to draw, which is why I made those illustrations(aren't they AWESOME?).

Thanks for all the support you give me when you choose to pick up my book.

Either someone with a good taste recommended you to give this book a try, or you looked at the flashy cover(designed by yours truly) and thought, 'THIS BOOK IS GOING TO BE AWESOME', only to realise that you need to buy the first part before this one. Lol.

You're in for a treat when you read the next one, which is going to come out soon, as I find that my writing improves with each book.

Now I know you guys like the adventures and pranks more than the descriptions, so I'll definitely keep that in mind while drafting out the rest of the series!

Best Wishes,

Khushi Goel

Look out for more of such
Intergalactic Space Adventures!!

Join Hazel and her friends
in their next quest in

HAZEL HALLEY AND THE QUEST FOR THE QUASAR

www.ingramcontent.com/pod-product-compliance
Lightning Source LLC
LaVergne TN
LVHW041210150826
845673LV00001B/349

* 9 7 9 8 8 9 0 6 7 9 9 8 7 *